MESMERIZED

Harry knew nothing of fashion, only that her gown was the color of deep claret, made of silk that looked almost black except where the direct light hit it and showed the richness of fine wine held up before a candle. The sleeves of her gown—well, there were hardly any sleeves, leaving her shoulders bare and a stretch of her upper arms equally unclothed to the top of her long gloves. In her light hair, Elizabeth wore a circlet of flowers all made of the same shimmering shade. Whenever she moved, the fabric changed, drawing his eye, glimmering, teasing. What was more intriguing—the swell of her breasts, the velvet of her arms, or the glimmer of her gown? Whichever it was, Harry found himself mesmerized by her beauty.

BOOK YOUR PLACE ON OUR WEBSITE AND MAKE THE READING CONNECTION!

We've created a customized website just for our very special readers, where you can get the inside scoop on everything that's going on with Zebra, Pinnacle and Kensington books.

When you come online, you'll have the exciting opportunity to:

- View covers of upcoming books
- Read sample chapters
- Learn about our future publishing schedule (listed by publication month *and author*)
- Find out when your favorite authors will be visiting a city near you
- Search for and order backlist books from our online catalog
- Check out author bios and background information
- Send e-mail to your favorite authors
- Meet the Kensington staff online
- Join us in weekly chats with authors, readers and other guests
- Get writing guidelines
- AND MUCH MORE!

**Visit our website at
http://www.kensingtonbooks.com**

AN IDEAL MATCH

Victoria Hinshaw

ZEBRA BOOKS
Kensington Publishing Corp.
http://www.kensingtonbooks.com

One

Elizabeth Drayton wrapped a second shawl around her black-clad shoulders and hurried down the staircase to the dimly lit drawing room. Warmth from the fire hardly penetrated the room's damp chill. Two candles flickered on the table, their flames lighting only a tiny circle in the murky gloom.

Bertha, Dowager Countess of Allward, mother of Elizabeth's deceased husband, glowered at the late arrival, her look of disapproval saying far more than words. Shivering, Elizabeth hastily sat on a straight-backed wooden chair, expecting an instant scold. Beside her sat Hester, the younger Countess of Allward, also draped in shapeless black, head bowed as she waited to read from a book of sermons, a daily ritual both at dawn and again after sunset. Three widows, locked in a cycle of grief, regret, and misery without relief.

The dowager frowned at Elizabeth but her words were harmless. "You may begin, Hester."

Hester began to read in a low monotone. Elizabeth hardly heard a word her sister-in-law muttered.

Ever since she and Reginald had come to Allward Manor six years ago, Elizabeth spent hours every day with these two bleak and bitter ladies. Her life had been even more circumscribed since Reginald died. One year, one month, and one week ago.

She was a virtual prisoner in this shadowy,

forbidding house, where the dark hangings of deep mourning had never been cast aside. The dowager required the presence of her two widowed daughters-in-law almost every moment of the day. Elizabeth could hardly go out for a walk on the moor. Even sitting in the library with a book was frowned upon. When they engaged in needlework, it was always mending or sewing shirts for the farm workers, nothing like the silk embroidery Elizabeth had learned as a girl.

Only rarely could she find time in secret to write a letter. She had arranged to receive her mail at the vicar's house when she found the dowager had opened a letter to Elizabeth from her cousin.

But now, the dreary routine would end very soon.

If only she could bear another few days, she would make her escape and learn to breathe freely. Teach herself to smile and laugh again.

But that thought brought her a tinge of renewed sadness. For she would have to leave Richard behind in this house of sorrow. Her nephew, the nine-year-old Earl of Allward, would miss her. And she would miss him very much. But not for long, she hoped.

"Elizabeth, you must read the poems next!" The dowager's grating tone broke into her thoughts. Not a word of the sermon had penetrated her head.

She took a book from the table and opened it at the marked page. She tipped it toward the meager light and started to read, her voice barely above a whisper.

"Beneath the bowing yews, upon the moonless plain . . . beside the weeping willows . . . gravestones mossy . . . came the hooded figure bent in sorrow . . ."

Though she spoke the words of the poem, Elizabeth's mind was far away. In a few days, if she calculated correctly, her cousins would arrive to take her away, whether the dowager wished her to go.

To Elizabeth, the dowager's life of self-negation and these repetitious recitals of self-improving tracts were hypocrisy of the highest degree. The elder Lady Allward constantly claimed her only interest was preserving the family heritage for Richard, but instead of caring for others, upholding the stewardship of the land, and honoring the memory of the two dead earls and Reginald—father, son, and brother—the dowager and Hester had turned their rightful mourning into a gloomy and self-indulgent obsession. And the way they treated the young earl, keeping him cooped up with books and unable to meet other children, why it was a disgrace! No child should have to live as Richard did because his grandmother's notions of raising a child were twisted and unnatural.

Elizabeth wished she could find some pity in her heart for the dowager. She had often tried to assuage her mother-in-law's heartache and misery, especially when she and Reginald had first arrived at Allward. Over the years, she had come to realize that Reginald's mother preferred to display her unhappiness at the expense of all else. The house remained draped in black, the chandeliers never fully lit.

The past year had been particularly stultifying. Without Reginald to talk with, Elizabeth felt herself shriveling inside. Without Reginald to buffer the strict regimen the dowager demanded, poor Richard was miserable. If Hester, Richard's mother, wished him a more vigorous life, she never said so. Only Elizabeth and the tutor, Owen Macneil, attempted to bring the boy some measure of cheer.

". . . the stony sepulchre forever sealed, and tears never more to cease."

When at last Elizabeth came to the end of the poem and put the book aside, she felt the dowager's eyes bore into her. Elizabeth raised her head and met the dark gaze directly.

The dowager's brow furrowed, her voice crackling with indignation. "You are not to leave Allward, Elizabeth. Your duty is to your memory of Reginald and to his family, not to your cousin." She drew a letter from her sleeve and waved it in the air. "This came for you today, and fortunately, Fox brought it to me. I regret that it is too late to prevent the arrival of this cousin of yours, but we will send her on her way the very next day."

Elizabeth studied her hands, suppressing her instant burst of resentment. Alice had followed her directions precisely and sent a letter the dowager was sure to intercept, as planned. It was the only way Elizabeth could devise that would prevent the elder Lady Allward from ordering Alice and her husband, Blaine Gifford, not to come.

Now Elizabeth needed to follow her own plan just as exactly. She drew a deep breath.

"It has been more than a year since Reginald was taken from us. I respect your right to spend the rest of your life mourning the deaths of your husband and sons. But I cannot do that. I shall go with my cousin and her husband and make my future in London."

"How dare you desecrate the memory of my son by turning away from his home and his legacy!" The dowager's hooded eyes glittered with menace.

Elizabeth was glad she had taken the precaution of having made a duplicate key to her room, for she would not be surprised if the dowager locked her in tonight. She needed to summon her firmest resolve.

"I do not consider it proper for you to intercept my letters. But since you have done so, then you know that I will be leaving in a few days."

"I do not wish to be defied, Elizabeth. You must not leave Allward."

Again, Elizabeth took a great sustaining breath, her heart pounding but her words utterly calm. "You will recall that I first met Reginald in London, married him there, and lived with him in town for several years before we came to Allward. I am going home to the years of my greatest joy with Reginald and to my family."

That was laying it on a bit thick, but Elizabeth hoped to deter a long argument that would only exhaust them and settle nothing. She had her own plans to put into effect, and nothing Reginald's mama said would stop her.

The Dowager Countess of Allward stood tall and glared at Elizabeth. "I do not approve of your ideas, Elizabeth. But if you leave Allward, do not expect ever to be permitted to return. Once you are gone, you are no longer part of my family. If that is what you wish, then I never want to see you again, here or anyplace else."

Elizabeth noted the expression that passed across Hester's face, a look of shock and horror. Then she looked at Elizabeth with what seemed to be a glimmer of admiration. Perhaps someday, Elizabeth thought, Hester would find her own way out of this dreadful existence. Once Richard entered Eton, perhaps Hester too might escape from the dowager's heavy hand.

"You may condemn me if you wish, but I believe you both would be better off if you tried to resume a more normal life, bring some light and activity into this dreary mausoleum."

"Enough!" The dowager shook a finger at Elizabeth, and her voice quivered with rage. "I have no wish in the world but to revere my husband's legacy and protect the honored name of this family."

Elizabeth shook her head. "And you are perfectly correct to do so. But I cannot stay here and watch you wither away."

She wanted to say more, much more, but she knew it would meet deaf ears. Sadly, she turned and climbed the stairs. There were few clothes she wanted to take along, but she needed to pack the little she had.

When Elizabeth entered the schoolroom, Mr. Macneil stood and bowed to her. Richard's glistening eyes and quivering lower lip made her wince, and she rushed to embrace his thin shoulders and press her cheek to his pale curls. He was a mere wisp of a boy, far too thin for good health. "Please do not be upset, Richard."

Mr. Macneil waited until she let the boy go. "Richard is distressed because the Dowager Lady Allward told us you would never be received at Allward again."

Richard pulled out of her arms and gazed into her face. "I wanted to tell her you would always be welcome at my house, because I know that Allward is really mine, not hers. But I was afraid she would get angrier. I was not brave enough. . . ."

"Richard, you did not lack courage. You know that Grandmama must be obeyed, so you did the proper thing. Once you go to Eton, I will see you there. Perhaps I will find a house in London where you and Mr. Macneil can come to visit. Would you like that?"

"Very much, Aunt Elizabeth."

"Then I shall be sure I find a place you will enjoy." She turned to Mr. Macneil and handed him a folded paper. "Here is the direction of my cousin in London. Please write to me there as soon as you have made plans for school. And make it as soon as possible." Elizabeth tried to convey the urgency she felt through pressing the tutor's hand. "Remember, both Richard's father and his uncle wanted him to attend Eton."

Mr. Macneil nodded. "I shall do my best, Mrs. Drayton. I have already written to a friend who is a fellow at the college to engage us some accommodations for the summer term beginning in April."

"Excellent." Elizabeth again hugged the boy. "It will be only a few weeks until I see you again, Richard. Until then, do everything your grandmama and Mr. Macneil tell you."

"I shall, Aunt Elizabeth."

She blew him one more kiss as she backed out of the door. Leaving him was the only part of her departure she regretted.

The dowager did not emerge from her bedchamber to bid Elizabeth's party good-bye. Only Hester accompanied them to the hall and wished them a good journey.

Elizabeth embraced her sister-in-law's slumping shoulders. "You must be sure that Richard goes to school soon, Hester. It will be good for him to go out into the world."

Hester looked forlorn. "I will miss him."

"But you must do what is best and what the last two earls planned for him."

A quarter hour later, Elizabeth rested her forehead against the window of her cousin's coach and watched Allward disappear behind a curve in the road. When she could no longer identify the stone wall surrounding the estate, she sank back on the soft cushions and gave a big sigh.

"You are relieved to be away from there, Lizzie?" Alice took Elizabeth's hand and squeezed it gently.

"Yes, I am."

"So am I. I have never felt less welcome in my life. And the food was inedible, for the most part."

The apparently napping Blaine opened one eye. "Do not worry, my pet. We will stop at an inn soon for a hearty meal."

Elizabeth tried to grin. "I believe you have missed your claret, Mr. Gifford."

"And my hock. And my brandy. And even a strong cup of coffee." He closed his eyes again and folded his hands across his waistcoat.

"How have you endured it all these years, Elizabeth?" Alice's voice was full of compassion.

"When Reginald was alive, I tried to find things to like about Allward, though the dowager has made it thoroughly bleak. She has a strong sense of preserving it for Richard, however, and I know she will not allow it to deteriorate. But not a flower blooms all spring and summer except a few wild bluebells in the woods. The child should have had a dog or at least a kitten. Until his tutor came, I was the only one who tried to bring a smile to his face with silly stories and games."

Alice shook her head. "That is no way to treat a child."

"Yes, I sympathize with the dowager, who lost her husband, then both of her sons. But I would expect her to be devoted to Richard's best interests. Instead, she tries to suppress all his boyish amusements. But before he died, Reginald made his mother renew her promise that the young earl would be enrolled at Eton. Hence the tutor."

"Will his grandmother really allow Richard to leave Allward?"

"I pray she will. I have encouraged Hester to insist.

It was the wish of his father that his son follow in his footsteps. I think the dowager sees it as her duty to the family because the old earl, her husband, went to school there too."

"Then she will probably let him go."

"I hope so. Richard needs contact with other boys. In fact, he needs to learn to be a boy, to counteract the influence of his grandmother's strict ideas. If he were to stay at Allward under her tutelage, Richard would be sure to break away eventually. He might even become a libertine of gigantic proportions after years of being stifled and molded to her narrow model."

"You mean the way the Prince of Wales reacted to his parents?"

"Exactly. If ever there was a model of how not to raise sons . . ." Elizabeth let her voice fade away.

Alice nodded vigorously. "No need to go into details! So tell me, dearest, what caused you to go to Allward? I have forgotten why you and Reginald went to live there. You had your own life in London, did you not?"

"Reginald felt it was his duty to take care of the family estates on behalf of his mother and Richard. The boy was only four years old when his father died." Elizabeth wished she had voiced her opposition to Reginald's move to Allward after his brother died. But, like so many things in her life, she had meekly agreed to the plans of others.

Blaine opened his eyes again. "I did not have much time for inspection, but it appears Reginald did an excellent job managing the place."

"His greatest regret was that he could not counteract his mother's schemes for Richard. Four years of age is not the time when a child can comprehend his future responsibilities. Once he became Earl of Allward, the dowager refused to allow him to see other boys of his age, and she set up a strict regimen of lessons in moral imperatives as well as Greek, Latin, and the classics."

"Did his mother not object?"

"Not that I heard. Perhaps you do not understand what it is to live with a person like the dowager. I did not object to her routines either. If Reginald's protests were futile, what could I do?"

Alice still looked disgruntled. "But you had to give up your old lives to hide away in Yorkshire."

Elizabeth nodded, relieved that her cousin understood so clearly. "Yes, but I refuse to dwell upon it now. I am free, and I intend to find a new life."

Alice laced her gloved fingers into Elizabeth's hand. "You know we want you to live with us."

"That very thought has comforted me and truly kept me going in the last year. I cannot tell you how much your help means to me, though I do not think I have to be dependent on anyone. I have adequate resources, do I not, Mr. Gifford?"

"We are family. Please call me Blaine. I repeat Alice's invitation, cousin Elizabeth. We would love to have you stay with us in Brook Street as long as you wish. Or at Gifford Manor, which I believe you and Reginald visited some years ago, did you not?"

"We did. And a lovely place it is. I have fond memories of our stay there—in July, I believe it was. The gardens were lovely."

She leaned forward a little to encourage him to continue on the subject of her finances.

He smiled, apparently recognizing her desire. "I have engaged a man to superintend the inventory and care of the assets left you by Reginald. You may be assured that your annual income will exceed four or five thousand a year."

Alice's gasp was matched by Elizabeth's.

"You do not mean that!"

"Indeed I do, cousin Elizabeth. Your husband was a very wealthy man. He apparently turned a small inheritance from an aunt into a considerable fortune by clever investments, good sense, and sound management."

"I had no idea it was so much." Elizabeth felt the tears gather in her eyes.

"Nor did his mother, I suspect. Before we departed London, I took the liberty of checking into the condition of the Allward estates, and they have been run well in the last dozen years."

"Then the dowager and Hester have no immediate needs for an infusion of funds?"

"No, indeed. As you requested, I did not make it known to anyone that the terms of Reginald's will left only a small legacy to his mother and nothing to his brother's family. As it should be for a second son who inherits none of the entailed family estates. I am well acquainted with the solicitors who supervise the trusts held for Richard, and they assure me the boy's future is well looked after."

"Thank you, cousin Blaine. I cannot tell you how much it means to me to know you are taking care of my interests."

"Think nothing of it, my dear."

Alice was still open-mouthed in amazement. "You did not know how much you had, Lizzie?"

"I knew only that the remaining assets, after the will's terms were fulfilled, were left to me. The dowager had no idea how much that might be and never inquired. I think she thought Reginald had only enough to live on. That he made investments never occurred to her, and I said nothing."

Blaine gave a chuckle. "Reginald had things arranged perfectly with his London representatives, hidden in plain sight. When I brought them a letter from you, they cooperated immediately."

Alice's face shone with glee. "Then Lizzie, you will be a wealthy widow! If you do not mind my making light of it, you will be much in demand in the marriage mart, or should I say, the second marriage mart!"

Elizabeth shivered in horror. "Do not be a henwit, Alice. I have about as much interest in marrying again as I have in jumping off London Bridge."

"Nonsense. You must find another husband. And you will be ardently pursued, dearest. We shall have a merry time escorting you to London routs as your chaperones, if you allow us the pleasure."

"I find the idea ludicrous. It has been years since I attended anything remotely like a London party. I would not remember how to behave, and your fun would be short lived."

"We shall have a merry time assembling a wardrobe for you. No more blacks, Elizabeth. With your pale complexion and blond hair, we will need to find just the right colors to bring out the bloom in your cheeks. I have a superior modiste, Madame Kuony, who keeps me *au courant* with all the latest fashions.

She will love having you to dress."

Blaine, who had sunk back in his corner, muttered a few words. It sounded to Elizabeth as though he was remarking about the modiste's bank account.

But Alice chattered on, oblivious. "I see you in many shades of green to match your eyes."

"My eyes are not green. They are gray, quite without color."

Alice gave a little giggle. "Do not contradict me, Elizabeth. You can see your eyes only in a mirror. Even in the dim light of this carriage I can see they are distinctly green." She poked at her husband. "Is that not so, my dear?"

Blaine groaned and mumbled something.

"You see? He thinks they are green also."

Elizabeth thought nothing of the kind, but it was hopeless to argue. And what did it matter if Alice thought her eyes were purple? She owed everything to her cousin, and it appeared the best way to repay her was to give Alice her wish to introduce Elizabeth to her friends.

Alice continued to tease her about abundant marriage prospects on the horizon, and Elizabeth responded in kind. It was only later, when they ran out of conversation, that Elizabeth gazed out of the coach window at the springtime scene and let her mind wander. The farther from Allward they traveled, the better she felt. Even the February sunshine tried to break through a thin layer of clouds and bring brighter prospects to the road ahead. Alice's cheek rested on the cushions, and her even breathing told Elizabeth she had joined her husband in a little nap.

Elizabeth's head was full of her secret dreams. For several months, the vision had been there in her brain, the vision of a house, her very own house. She could see its vague outlines on a slope above the Thames, far upstream from the city, in Surrey or even Berkshire. It would be a house of modest proportions with enough land for an orchard and a garden. She had no idea where the mental picture came from, yet it had a powerful hold on her, even more powerful because it was her secret, unshared with anyone.

Elizabeth had been a little less than honest with Blaine, for she had known enough of Reginald's affairs to know that his holdings were substantial. Poor Reginald had become ever more compulsive, more like his mother, if the truth were told. Reginald gave up his chosen life for his family, and his mother never appreciated it. As far as she was concerned, no sacrifice was too great to make in the name of the earls of Allward.

But Reginald had his own kind of rebellion. Unknown to his mother, many of the hours he had spent at his desk at Allward were devoted to his investments and other business interests beyond his nephew's estate.

Too many hours. Almost as though he had taken refuge in the estate office to avoid contact with the ladies. To be honest, she and Reginald had grown far apart in the years spent at Allward. Under the influence of his mother, he became introspective and bad tempered. He lost interest in having children, for which Elizabeth had an abiding regret.

Of course, that might be one advantage to marrying again, if she found the right match. She was still young enough to have children. But any potential husband would probably come with a family already, several children grieving for a lost mother. That might not be the kind of family she needed.

No, better to be independent, as shocking as that sounded. Not that she would disclose such a scandalous thought to anyone, even Alice. No one would expect her to establish her very own household, but that was exactly what Elizabeth intended to do.

She was determined to have her own establishment, one where she could express her own tastes. Strange as it seemed, she had never had a house of her own. When she left her parents, she lived in Reginald's house, with furniture and servants chosen by him. At the time, it had not occurred to her to change a single thing. Then, she lived at Allward where the dowager allowed no deviation from her austere choice of furnishings—dark, sparse and mostly uncushioned, as if a soft sofa would be evidence of disrespect for the lost men of the family.

Elizabeth's house would be full of light, with soft colors and plush sofas, full of flowers and the sweet scents of rosewater and lavender *potpourri*. She would have a fortepiano and begin to play again. A sunny nook could be outfitted for painting watercolors, something she had not set her hand to since she left her father's house. And she would have a well-cushioned chaise near a large oil lamp for reading. It would be her haven from the world.

Alice awakened, snuggled near, and put her head on Elizabeth's shoulder. She whispered so as not to disturb her still-napping husband. "Lizzie, I have just thought of two perfect gentlemen for you. I cannot wait to introduce you."

Elizabeth bit back an instant refusal. That would be no way to reward Alice and Blaine for rescuing her. Instead, she sighed and feigned a nap herself.

A few weeks of the London social scene, and she could withdraw gracefully. The notion of finding another husband made her shudder.

Two

Mr. Harry Marlowe sent a longing look toward his desk where a delicate fern lay beside his pencils and a half-done sketch of the single frond, a drawing that was not nearly good enough. In the golden glow of the oil lamp, his attempt at an exact botanical representation appeared pitifully childish.

He glanced back at the mirror and gave his neck-cloth a little twitch, then strode to the desk and crumpled the drawing. He would start over in the morning with a fresh specimen.

Harry almost groaned when he heard his man open the door and greet his brother-in-law, Sir James Powell. On the stroke of ten, just as promised. Why had Harry not refused this useless invitation to another dull party? Another gathering where his sister Faith would introduce him to a series of ladies, always hoping he would show a spark of interest in one of them. She knew he had no intention of marrying again, yet no amount of protesting slowed her earnest efforts to find him the ideal match. Whether a ball or a musicale for hundreds or a dinner for twenty, Faith always had some lady in tow, a prospect for his potential approval.

Harry greeted the baronet with a wry grin. "G'evening, James. I hope that the earlier we arrive, the more promptly we can depart."

Sir James did not remove his cloak. "I believe

Faith has promised us to more than one hostess this evening."

Harry sighed aloud, took up his hat and gloves, and followed Sir James to the waiting barouche.

Several hours later, as they entered the third of the evening's entertainments, Harry promised himself he would do no more than pay his respects to the hostess, thank Faith and James for their company, and promptly walk home. Though the party had gone from house to house by carriage, Harry's lodgings were only a few streets away.

Before Harry left, he wanted to see Lady Simpson's recently installed conservatory. Slipping away from a conversation in which he had been only a peripheral participant, he asked directions from a bewigged footman. And for good measure, he lifted two goblets brimming with champagne from the servant's tray and followed his directions to the conservatory. Might as well enjoy Lady Simpson's hospitality before he wished her a good evening. He was thirsty enough to drink a whole bottle.

The glass-roofed room was dimly lit but obviously a fine example of the latest modern improvements in building glass houses. Harry stood for a moment inhaling the warm, moist scent of the plants. He set one of the goblets on the edge of a plinth holding a graceful palm and took a sip from the other glass, letting the tart wine trickle down his throat. Overhead he could see an *Allagoptera arenaria* and an *Astrocaryum mexicanum*, large specimens indeed, and below them a bougainvillea with its bright bracts of color.

A lady's soft voice broke into his observations. "Excuse me. I fear I have wandered too far."

Harry turned and saw her figure silhouetted against the lights of the salon, a few diamonds twinkling in her hair as she glanced behind her. Her voice, musical and low, touched a chord within him, though he could not yet see her face clearly.

"Lady Simpson recently built this conservatory, which I have come to see. Perhaps you have done the same without exactly realizing where you were going."

"Perhaps." She took a few steps into the conservatory and gazed around her.

He reached for the oil lamp control and turned it up.

She was lovely, dressed in dove gray satin that shimmered in the glow. Her face was luminous and beautiful, but her eyes carried a hint of caution.

He bowed to her. "I regret that we have not been introduced. I am Harry Marlowe, at your service."

She gave him a tiny nod and an equally small curtsy. "I am Mrs. Drayton. I am afraid I feel rather out of place here."

To his eye, she looked perfectly in place. He searched his memory for a fellow named Drayton but came up with no one of his acquaintance, not even a name from the roster of the club.

He bowed again. "Mrs. Drayton, I am pleased to make your acquaintance. And I must say you do not look out of place at all. Are you new to town?"

"Yes, and I am not very comfortable among so many strangers."

"I sympathize more than you know. Frequently I am not so comfortable at balls myself."

"I came with my cousin, Mrs. Gifford, and her husband."

He did not recall any Giffords either. "I arrived in the company of my brother-in-law and my sister, Sir James and Lady Powell."

"I'm afraid I do not know . . ."

"Then, since we have no acquaintances in common to vouch for my character, I will offer my own assessment for your evaluation. I am a man of the highest integrity, of all that is virtuous, and of honorable intentions."

He was delighted to see a smile curve her lips and light her eyes.

Harry took up the goblet of champagne and offered it to her. "Mrs. Drayton, hearing no demur from my list of sterling attributes, could I invite you to investigate our hostess's botanical specimens with me? I suspect the path leads us in a circle."

She accepted the glass of champagne and nodded her assent. "I am sure this is rather improper, but I admit to being curious about why Lady Simpson would want banana plants growing in her house."

He offered her his arm, and she placed her hand lightly under his elbow. "Mrs. Drayton, now I am curious myself. Not everyone could recognize a member of the *Musaceae* family."

"Oh, am I incorrect? To me, that looks very much like a plant I saw at Kew, the one with the big, red flower hanging down. Is that not so?"

"You are quite correct. A banana plant. If you will excuse another question, how did you come to visit the king's collections at Kew Gardens?"

She gave a little sniff of laughter. "My cousins are determined to show me every curiosity in and near London. They are really very kind, and I have been enjoying myself, except when they insist that I accompany them to . . . Oh, I sound like a mewling child."

"I myself have experienced overweening relatives at times. So, I very much understand. One feels ungrateful resenting the insistence of others to act in what they define as one's best interests."

"Yes, I can see that you do understand."

"I do, but I shall not further burden you with my

philosophizing. Instead, shall I bore you by reciting the genus and species of these plants?"

She stopped and turned her face up to his. "You know the names of all these?"

The light seemed to twinkle in her eyes, and her parted lips seemed so velvety soft that Harry was tempted to lean down and kiss her. Instead, he cleared his throat and chuckled. "Perhaps not every one, but that one is a *Brahea dulcis,* known as a rock palm, and there is a *Butia capitata,* a jelly palm from Brazil. Botany is rather an interest of mine."

"I see. Then I should like to hear more." She sipped the last of her champagne. "I never tried champagne until a few weeks ago. And I am afraid I like it far too much for my own good."

"I admit to a similar fondness, Mrs. Drayton. It is particularly delicious when imbibed in good company."

She smiled and stepped back. He feared he had gone a bit too far. He gestured to a flower nestled under the palm fronds. "This little bloom is a *Pelargonium capitatum.*"

She had just taken his arm again when they heard a group of people approaching the conservatory. She stiffened, her eyes wide.

"Thank you," she whispered and rushed off ahead of him.

Harry figured she did not want to be found here with him alone and so continued his stroll on the circular path, which kept him mostly concealed from the others. Near the doorway, he saw Mrs. Drayton waiting for a group of five or six laughing partygoers to enter. They were too preoccupied to notice her in the shadows and when they passed a few feet away from her, she hurried out of the conservatory and back through the salon toward the party. In a moment, Harry followed her, also unnoticed by the others.

As he sauntered back toward the noise of the crowd, he gave a mocking laugh to the empty salon. How ironic that the first woman who captured even an iota of his interest was married. Just one of those silly quirks of fate.

Abruptly he realized he was about to run into Mrs. Fitzmaurice-Smythe. He stopped just in time to avoid knocking the gold turban from her head.

"Oh, Mr. Marlowe, I was so hoping to encounter you this evening."

He supposed he was getting just what he deserved for not watching where he was going. "Good evening, Mrs. Fitzmaurice-Smythe." Unfortunately, the woman always wanted the same thing.

"Prudence is in the ballroom. I know she would be most delighted to have a dance with you."

"I'm afraid I was just going to depart, as I have promised to meet Lord Norwell at"—he guessed at the time—"half past one. I must make haste. I am so sorry. My very best regards to Miss Fitzmaurice-Smythe." He backed away as he spoke.

She sputtered as he bowed deeply and left without looking back.

Elizabeth's pounding pulse slowed a little as she entered the ballroom. From the empty salon, she moved into the noisy throng of people without noticing a single head turning in her direction. The scraping of chairs, the clamor of a hundred voices, some high-pitched and some deep bass, many cackling like a flock of fowl, assailed her ears. The farther into the swarm she went, the warmer it became, making her throat dry, her breath short.

Was she lucky enough to have escaped attention?

Despite her shattered composure, she kept a pleasant expression on her face and looked forward, trying to appear as though she were hurrying to meet a friend.

Ahead, the musicians tuned up for another set of dances. Time to find a sheltered spot out of the way of gentlemen looking for partners. To that end, she headed for the refreshment room, nodding to a woman she distinctly remembered meeting but whose name did not come to mind.

At last she gained a quiet corner and sank onto a chair beside two elderly ladies, one buxom, the other reedy and gaunt, prattling behind their fans. They did not glance in her direction.

Safe at last.

Whatever had drawn her to that conservatory she would never know. Mr. Marlowe had been all that was kind, but if she had been seen there with him, what tales would have been reported to his wife? A nice man like him must be married. She could hear the gossip. *Mrs. Drayton, that widow new to town, is very fast, losing no time in seeking out an assignation in a darkened garden room.* She felt more the beneficiary of good fortune than her own good sense.

She breathed deeply, willing her heart to slow down, her head to stop its pounding, and her hands to stop twisting the strings of her reticule.

Abruptly the ridiculousness of the situation struck her, and she almost laughed out loud. For her third excursion into the world of the ton, she had danced with two gentlemen whose company she hoped she would not have to endure again. And she had spent a quarter hour alone with a stranger who could have been anyone from a royal duke to a dustman in fine clothes.

Considering the dances, she should have ignored Alice's advice and sat out the sets. As for her other

adventure, she should have followed Alice's advice
not to wander off. If she and Mr. Marlowe had been
caught . . . but luckily she was in no danger of being
accused of seducing some other lady's husband.

Alice would be looking for her and would be full
of questions about where she had gone. She turned
to the two ladies.

"Might I bring you a cup of punch?"

The matron in the blue turban decorated with
peacock feathers smiled and raised her eyebrows to
the very brim of the blue wrap. "Why, how delightful, my dear. I was just thinking I would have
something."

Her companion nodded, setting a pair of pink
ostrich feathers to bobbing. "I too would appreciate a cup."

Elizabeth rose, curtsied to them, and went to the
punch bowl. When she had presented the drinks to
the ladies' effusive thanks, she returned and ladled
a portion for herself. She could hear the applause
marking the conclusion of the set, and through the
doorway, people were heading toward the refreshments. When she again took her seat, the blue
turban spoke.

"I believe we were introduced at Lady Hathorn's
last week, were we not?"

Elizabeth leaned toward her. "Yes, that is my recollection. I am Mrs. Drayton, a cousin of Mrs.
Gifford's."

The blue turban nodded toward her companion.
"You see, Hattie, I told you." She looked again at
Elizabeth. "I am Georgina Berwald, and this is my
dear friend, Mrs. Welk."

"I am sorry your names did not come immediately to mind. I have met so many people in the last
week, my head spins."

Mrs. Welk reached over and patted Elizabeth's

arm. "Do not refine upon it, my dear. If you and Alice will call on me on Thursday, we can enjoy a good coze and get to know one another."

Elizabeth had hardly finished her acceptance when Alice dashed up to their little group.

"I was worried about you, Elizabeth, afraid Mr. Higgs or Sir Jason had spirited you away to steal a kiss."

Mrs. Welk gave a hoot of laughter. "Sir Jason! Oh, famous! Georgie, can you envision Sir Jason sneaking Mrs. Drayton into his phaeton?"

Mrs. Berwald was trying not to choke on her punch. "That caper merchant! Would be a scene, I declare."

Alice laughed too. "I take it you do not believe Sir Jason is in the market for affection."

Mrs. Welk's pink feathers swayed from side to side. "He is far too fastidious. Kissing a lady might muss his perfectly arranged Waterfall cravat. Or disarrange his carefully windswept locks."

Alice drew Elizabeth up beside her. "I believe you ladies have the right of it. We can discuss some more eligible fellows when we meet. For now, my dear husband is more than eager to return home."

Elizabeth curtsied again to the two ladies and linked her arm through Alice's. Her near-indiscretion was securely undisclosed.

Harry gripped a long tweezers holding a tiny piece of wool. He passed it over the stamen of one plant and picked up a few grains of pollen. Carefully he moved it to another blossom and tapped it, gently dropping half a dozen nearly invisible particles on the pistil.

Just helping Mother Nature a little, doing what no bee would enter the greenhouse to accomplish for him. He had several experiments under way, trying to raise ferns in a glass box, forcing indoor peach trees to bear fruit, and miniaturizing a daisy.

Now he needed the cooperation of Mother Nature to bring a few sunny days to his seedlings. But at the moment, the cloud cover was heavy and there were signs of impending rainfall. He went outside and checked that his barrels were ready to catch any rainfall from the roof. Perhaps an unnecessary maneuver, but he always tried to water his plants with natural rainfall instead of water from the well. Only alter nature's way when it was absolutely necessary.

He walked into the library where Sir James sat frowning over his newspaper. One of the things he was most grateful for was his brother-in-law's offer to let him use the conservatory. Faith had wanted one badly a few years ago, but now, as long as James provided her with flowers for her dining table, she preferred to stay out of its humid air.

"Well, James, you look unhappy. The news is bad?"

"More of the same. You would think that after the many years of war ended in victory, the inhabitants of this kingdom would be grateful for the brilliance of our army and navy and provide employment for the veterans. Instead, we read on one page of the sad state of those who look for work and on the next of more extravagance from the Prince Regent or one of his useless brothers."

"Yes, it is most distressing. What are they saying in the Lords?"

"Nothing but platitudes that pass for debate." Sir James waved his hand as if dismissing the collective efforts of his fellow peers.

Harry assumed he would welcome a change of topic. "Do you know a Mr. Drayton?"

"What is the context of your question? Is he in the Commons or a man of the legal world?"

"I heard his name mentioned last night at Lady Simpson's ball."

James rubbed his jaw. "I must say the name sounds somewhat familiar, but I cannot say just why."

"Means nothing to me either."

Before James could ask him more questions, Harry began to tell him about his latest work in the conservatory.

When at last he left his brother-in-law to his newspaper, Harry walked back to his lodgings. He let his mind wander back to the lovely Mrs. Drayton, shimmering in her satin gown. Again he thought how ironic that Mrs. Drayton was a married woman. No one else had captured his briefest passing fancy. Yet this morning, Mrs. Drayton's shy smile invaded his first thoughts upon awakening.

He forced his mind back to the upcoming meeting to plan a voyage to South America to collect botanical specimens. More than nine years had passed since he returned from his youthful voyage, bringing with him seeds, plants growing in barrels, an amazing collection. In subsequent years, he cataloged the material and prepared and read several papers to the Royal Horticultural Society. To his gratification, he had engaged the regard of a number of influential men in botany.

His late wife's illness started him on his path. If she had been a hardy soul, he would have continued in the merchant marine and not pursued his interest in plants. But once he was married and Caroline proved so frail, he had to stay close to her. No more voyages.

She had died just as news of Wellington's victory at Waterloo arrived, almost two years ago. Where had the time gone? He spent a few days each month working at Kew with fellow devotees, particularly a few who shared his attachment to bromeliads from Brazil. For months they had been talking of another voyage, venturing deep into the jungles along the Amazon. In many ways, he wanted to go, to see again the regions he had explored. He knew so much more today than he had as a youth.

In other ways, Harry preferred to stay put. No matter how good the assistants he engaged to continue his various projects, many experiments would wither without his patient, personal care. He would have to move everything from Faith's, for she would not care to have some young student running loose in her house several times a week. Two years seemed like a very long time to be away.

Before Alice came downstairs, Elizabeth slipped away from the breakfast room, leaving Blaine to his newspaper. Elizabeth wanted to write in her diary, or more accurately, she wanted to think carefully about her encounter last night with Mr. Marlowe, whose image had haunted her dreams. He was the only gentleman she had met in London who had spoken with anything approaching normal civility, as though she was a person and not a body to be ogled or a purse to be plucked. But because they had not been properly introduced, she knew nothing about him and had no one to ask. She felt sure he was married, so how could she explain their acquaintance? If he was not married, all Alice would need was the mention of his name to have him thoroughly investigated. Alice's sources of information were formidable, and she would never believe Elizabeth was only curious.

Why did she feel an attraction to Mr. Marlowe? She knew nothing about him, just as he knew nothing

about her. For all she knew, he was married with a
dozen children and several mistresses.

She sat at her table and opened her writing desk.
She had purchased the silk-bound book of blank
pages at a stationer's across from the inn where she
had spent her first night of freedom from Allward.
The first seven pages were filled with her flood of
emotions upon leaving Richard and Mr. Macneil,
and her feelings about the dowager and Hester.
Her memories of Reginald had flowed onto another ten pages or so. Since then, her musing had
almost exclusively dealt with her desire to find a
modest house where she could pursue her interests
in painting and gardening, perhaps have a few
parish ladies in for tea, and read in silence whatever
she chose to pick up. No one to censure her books
or periodicals, no one to require recitation of improving tracts, no one to forbid her to choose a
new rose for the arbor.

Several pages toward the end recorded all her pur-
chases, and as she looked at them, she was amazed to
see how profligate she had become. Who needed
stockings by the dozen? Or six parasols?

Alice had kept her busy the past two weeks since
they had arrived in London. Elizabeth had but few
hours to herself here and there because there were
calls to make, calls to receive, shopping, outings in
the park, long hours of preparation for being seen.
It was certainly not the prison Allward had become,
but neither was she the mistress of her own time, a
state she earnestly desired.

Now that she sat before a blank page in her
diary, Elizabeth was not certain what she wanted
to write. She had already repeated her feelings
about independence, listed more than once all
the reasons for living alone, declared her purpose
again and again. She had enumerated the diffi-

culties involved in fulfilling her quest and had cataloged the impediments to carrying through her plan, even to the mundane nuisance of having no one to accompany her on visits to available properties.

Alice was much too busy managing her own social life, as well as that of her husband and of Elizabeth. There were the absolutely necessary errands every day, whether for fittings at the dressmakers or to choose a bonnet in the latest shade, another pair of gloves to add to the dozen she already had, or to acquire some other trifle she could not exist without having immediately. There were sights to be seen, curiosities to be visited, all of immediate importance, they said, to a lady being introduced to the ton.

Elizabeth was unable to decide whether all this frenetic activity was the result of Alice's natural exuberance or part of a plot she and Blaine hatched to keep Elizabeth from beginning her house hunting.

Whatever the motivation, such was the result. Though Elizabeth had a list of five suitable houses from Mr. Lytton, her man-of-business, she had not yet seen any of them. After several weeks of trying, she had almost given up. Obviously, she needed a new plan, for it was clear neither Alice nor Blaine was willing to assist her.

Not that they outright declined their assistance, no indeed. It was much more difficult than that. They would agree to go with her, only to find some other activity more pressing, or the carriage needed a minor repair, or the weather was poor, or their driver had been promised the afternoon off duty. Elizabeth wondered at the brilliant series of excuses they managed to concoct. Every little thing was a pretext to postpone the excursion.

She had only a vague idea of exactly what she

wanted in a new home. She thought she might be happier some distance from town, farther than Chelsea. But not too far either, for she thought she would enjoy attending various events in London, meetings of learned societies, perhaps, or presentations by eminent men of letters.

Until she actually saw a few houses and had a basis for comparison, she felt at a disadvantage in describing her needs. To find a house, she had to look around, not just sit here in her bedchamber and fuss about it.

But first there was another shopping excursion with Alice, and, after shopping, there were more gatherings to endure, more noise and strangers jabbering about nothing. And, no doubt, more prospective suitors. How could Alice have so many friends who knew men on the lookout for a wife?

Elizabeth sighed and closed her journal. If necessary, she could engage a companion, a lady who could be paid to accompany her in a hired carriage. Yes, unless Alice and Blaine yielded, that was precisely what she would do.

Three

Each day when the callers arrived, Elizabeth felt like a large china doll on display, perched in the middle of the room. The gentlemen circled around her, moving from Alice near the door, to the plate of sweets in one corner, to conversations among themselves in the other two. From time to time, as they completed one circuit and began another, they commented to her about the weather.

Sir Ennis never missed an opportunity. "Lovely spring day. Lovely."

Mr. Higgs had a deep, booming voice that matched the way he always spoke in negatives. "Not that it could not clear later . . ."

By contrast, the constant cheeriness of Sir Jason aggravated her for its inanity. "I always say, it is a sad day when Jason Bowman cannot find a beam of sunshine, however imaginary it might turn out to be . . ."

Weather, endless talk of weather. Was it raining? How hard?

Would it rain? When?

Would it stop raining? How soon?

Sometimes, she wished to stamp her foot and say, "It is spring. It rains in the spring. Every year. Please select a new topic of conversation." But, of course, she said nothing, just listened to the idiocy of it all and tried to smile.

She took to studying the men's clothing. Some, like Mr. Darrow, dressed well, with obvious care but a lack of ostentation. Others were fastidiously showy, displaying bright colors and shiny brass buttons. Sir Ennis always wore a noisy handful of fobs that clanked with his every step.

There were the cravats so stiff with starch they could slice an unwary fellow's neck. Lord Concannon's was tied so high he had to lean over to see below him, but it mostly covered his prominent Adam's apple, which looked like a billiard ball stuffed into the middle of a hollow cue.

They all had their individual style of greeting. Sir Ennis performed a low, sweeping bow with his leg extended out in front of him, as though he also swept off a plumed hat in a broad gesture from the royal courts of a hundred years ago. Others, like Mr. Gerber, made a shallow bow, probably trying to keep his corsets from creaking.

The ladies who came, usually later in the day, seemed to fall into several categories. Some were curious about her as a new arrival to their circle. They often had questions that bordered on the impolite, but not unkind. Some assessed her status compared with their friends and relations, both male and female, who might be searching for a match. Was she competition or a ripe plum to pluck?

Finally, there were those eager to pick up some juicy *on-dit* to pass along to their acquaintances later. Elizabeth could imagine them saying, "Did you notice Mrs. Drayton's hair? She looks very countrified, but I wager she will succumb to Alice's man before the month is out." Or perhaps they spoke of her reticence, whether she was able to carry a conversation past two exchanges.

What did it matter? She had no desire to make a splash in their social fountain. She was here as a guest, and it would be discourteous of her not to comply with Alice's style of life after Alice and Blaine had endured the long trip to Allward to rescue her. She tried to smile and was always polite, but she feared she would be of little interest to society after a week or two.

But she was wrong. The callers kept coming, and she gradually warmed to the experience, as she grew to know a few of them better.

One afternoon a few days after she had made her dangerous voyage into Lady Simpson's conservatory, Elizabeth sat with Alice and her husband's great-aunt, Lady Adeline Lynden. Everyone knew her as Lady Addie, charming but unwilling to admit she was hard of hearing. She had a tendency to recite her pedigree frequently, though she often got the names mixed up, not to mention the centuries. She was certain she could trace her family back farther than Mary, Queen of Scots, though when she arrived at Mary, she became so entranced with stories of the tragic queen, she usually forgot the family.

"Can you imagine sitting with Bess, stitching one fancy tapestry after another for year after year? What did the two women talk about? Poor Mary, confined in luxury, while old Shrewsbury tried to get out of paying for her entourage . . ."

Arlen, Alice's butler, interrupted. "Lady Powell."

Alice stood and welcomed the new arrival while Elizabeth made a mental note to read more about Mary's life.

When they were settled again, Lady Powell turned to Elizabeth and smiled. "Alice and I were in school together at Miss Prout's. I believe you also attended her school a few years later?"

"Yes, my father always thought that Alice had

perfect manners and that I needed to follow her example."

"I saw some of Mary's fine needlework preserved at Chatsworth," Lady Addie said.

Alice moved her chair closer to Lady Addie. "Is that so?"

Elizabeth felt a little shudder at the memory of all the mending she did at Allward. The dowager did not believe in wasting time on decorative tapestries. "I have not done any real needlework for many years."

"Nor have I," Lady Powell said, "I had more than my fill of it at school."

Alice chuckled. "I must say I liked doing my samplers better than French or lessons in history."

"History!" Lady Addie nodded her head vigorously. "Yes, Mary was one of the great figures in our history. Tragic, though, very tragic . . ."

"I hear you are new to London, Mrs. Drayton," Lady Powell spoke softly.

Elizabeth tried to match her tone. "Yes, although I lived here for several years before I moved to Yorkshire. But my late husband and I lived very quietly. We rarely went about in Society."

Lady Addie continued her pronouncements. "English history would have been quite different if Mary had taken the throne."

Alice, Lady Powell, and Elizabeth all nodded and smiled at Lady Addie.

The pattern continued for another quarter hour, and from time to time, Elizabeth was moved to laughter at the incongruity of it all. When her guests had taken their departure, Alice collapsed on the sofa. "I truly adore Blaine's great-aunt, but I declare it is impossible to carry on a coherent conversation when she is around."

Elizabeth carried her teacup to the tray. "She

does not seem to mind that few of her remarks bring any response."

"I am convinced the dear lady does not hear a single word we say, Elizabeth."

"How very difficult it must be for her."

"Oh, not anymore. It has been this way for as long as I can remember. Blaine takes her for an airing in the park every week, and he says she has been a little batty since he was a child."

Elizabeth sat down again and smoothed out her skirt. "Lady Powell is very amiable."

"Yes, Faith and I do not see one another often enough, except at the large *soirées*. I am delighted she called to meet you. I believe she intends to introduce you to her brother."

Elizabeth prevented herself from frowning with some effort. Why had she not guessed there would be yet another tiresome man to be met?

Harry inspected each seedling in Faith's greenhouse and pronounced himself satisfied. He plucked a few blossoms and took them to the breakfast room, hoping to tuck them into a vase and be off without waking his sister. Sir James had long ago left to meet his colleagues for luncheon.

Faith, to his surprise, was seated at the breakfast table.

"I thought you usually had your toast in your bedchamber."

"Oh, Harry, I am delighted to see you. Sit and have a cup of tea with me."

"I am due at Sir Joseph's—"

"He is only in Soho Square; it will not take you more than five minutes to walk there. I have some news of interest to you."

He took a chair, though he sincerely doubted that

his sister would have any news that would interest him. She was a clever puss, always had been, but her main interests were involved with Society, its ins and outs, ups and downs. She was quick to catch on to the latest trends . . . and lately she had become almost obsessed with one thing.

"I have found the perfect lady for you."

Her main purpose in life seemed to be finding him a wife, a wife he neither wanted nor needed. Since her youngest son went off to school, she had little else to occupy her rather formidable energies. Harry was thoroughly content just as he was.

Her voice broke in again. "Are you not going to ask any questions?"

He drained his teacup. "I know you will tell me, no matter if I ask or not."

"Harry! You have become too rude to deserve a wife."

If only she would believe that. "Oh?" He shoved his hand through his hair, pushing an unruly strand into place.

"Stop that! You mustn't disturb your windswept arrangement. I declare, it takes James more than a half hour to get that look just so."

"My hair truly *was* arranged by the wind and my mussing it."

"No, Harry, that is too . . . but wait. You have distracted me again. You must listen to me, Harry. This lady is very sweet. She is a widow who has been living in Yorkshire—"

He could not prevent a chuckle escaping.

"What are you laughing at?"

"The vision of a woman I once met who hailed from Yorkshire. She smoked a pipe."

"Wherever did you—wait! Do not try to divert me anymore, you abominable wretch! This lady does nothing of the kind. She is perfectly refined."

And shopping for a husband, he thought. "I see."

"Sarcasm is hardly necessary. I just thought you would like to know that tonight, I will introduce you to—"

"I may be at Sir Joseph's rather late. I thought I would skip tonight's social events."

"You cannot. This lady is rich, so she is bound to have many admirers dangling after her before long."

"You mean there are other men in London who are not attached to a female? From the way you talk, I thought I must be the rarest bird in town."

Her pout was instantaneous. "Harry, you are not kind. You know I have only your best interests at heart. You must understand. . . ."

"I understand, my dear conniving sister. But I have told you over and over again that I am quite happy just as I am."

"Surely you miss Caroline."

"Yes, I miss her. But I have become rather attached to my solitude. Besides, I have you and James."

That brought a smile to her face. "Please say that you will come with us to the Benton's tonight."

"I cannot. I am planning to attend a talk at the Royal Horticultural Society this evening." He turned to a footman. "I will be leaving in a moment."

Her face clouded, and she clasped her hands to her bosom. "Oh, Harry, no. I promised Alice. . . ."

"Alice who?"

"Alice Gifford."

He'd heard that name recently, but he was not sure where. He nodded to the footman, who had come back with Harry's things.

Faith went on quickly. "The widow is her cousin. I met her yesterday. She is both very pretty and amiable."

"I am afraid I—"

"I do so want you to meet Mrs. Drayton."

He halted at the door. "Mrs. Drayton, you say?" *So she is a widow!*

"Have you already made her acquaintance?"

"Why, ah, no. Of course not." He felt a little twinge of pleasure creep up his spine.

"She is very pretty."

Yes, he remembered. Even in the dim light, she was graceful and radiant, with creamy skin and a fine figure. She had a sweetly melodious voice. . . .

He took his hat and stick. "Well, if you insist. Perhaps I can meet you a bit before midnight. Where did you say you are going?"

"The Benton's, in Brook Street. Harry, I think you will be glad you made the effort."

As he walked briskly toward Soho Square, he felt lighthearted. It was breezy, but one could feel the promise of warmth in the air. Trees were budding and even against the noise of the traffic, he could hear an occasional bird singing.

At 10:00 P.M., Brook Street was clogged with a long line of carriages waiting to deliver their be-jeweled guests to the door of the Benton mansion. As they waited their turn to alight, Alice placed her hand on Elizabeth's arm.

"Promise me you will not wander away again, Elizabeth. We worried about you the other night. I have a charming man in mind to introduce to you this evening."

Elizabeth had an instant mental picture of another burly squire with a thick neck and thinning hair, but she summoned a smile. "Perhaps we can make a bargain, cousin dear. If I promise to be cordial to your prospect this evening, will you and Blaine accompany me to visit some properties next week, without any more excuses?"

"But why are you so anxious to leave us, Elizabeth? Are you not comfortable?"

Elizabeth drew a steadying breath. "I have explained to you why I wish to have my own establishment. Surely we need not go over that ground again?"

Alice turned to her husband. "What do you say, my dear? Are you available Thursday?"

Blaine gave a snort of laughter. "Nothing I cannot postpone, if you two are in agreement."

Alice pursed her lips. "That means I will keep my eye on you all evening, Elizabeth. I expect you to dance a full set with my protégé, agreed?"

Elizabeth grinned. "Assuming that the gentleman is disposed to ask me to join him."

When the carriage door opened and a footman let down the step, Alice grabbed Elizabeth's elbow. "I shall hold you to your word."

Elizabeth gave Alice a playful poke. "My word is good. Make sure yours is the same!"

Fully half an hour passed before the three of them managed to negotiate the foyer, to visit the retiring room to leave their cloaks, to penetrate the jam on the stairs, and to be announced at the door of the ballroom.

Elizabeth's glee at extracting the promise from her cousin was as frayed as her hair must be. She tried to edge closer to a mirror to check her curls, once carefully arranged but now spoiled by a dozen brushes with a stray sleeve or someone's careless gesture. To her surprise and relief, it did not look too untidy. She pushed a few drifting wisps into place and shrugged away her concern.

Now she had merely to endure another few hours of the noisy, overheated ballroom and keep a smile pasted on her face for the latest swain—when and if he managed to make his way through the crush and find Alice. In fact, she hoped the gentleman would not make it at all.

It seemed this gilded ballroom held the only ton party of the evening. Even after the early departures, there would be a fresh onslaught when the opera finished. Perhaps by staying with Alice and not finding a potted palm behind which to conceal herself, she would still be protected from the new presentation, for how anyone found one another in here she would never know. Just another of Society's unfathomable paradoxes. Hostesses prided themselves on the intensity of their squeezes. The more uncomfortable the guests, the stuffier the air, the bigger the gathering's success.

In the crowd, Alice's prospect might not find them. However, she noted, as a thin-faced gentleman waved at her from across the room, she would have to see a few of Alice's previous aspirants. Nevertheless, anything was worth the promise of house hunting tomorrow.

Later, after dancing three sets, each with a man Alice had introduced her to in the last weeks, Elizabeth was relieved to take a seat beside Alice and wiggle her toes inside her satin slippers. Her first partner, Sir Jason Bowman, had not stepped on her once. The second, the corpulent Mr. Higgs, despite making numerous missteps and snarling the entire line at one point, managed to avoid her feet. But her third collaborator, Mr. Darrow, bluff and hearty, proved himself adept only at crushing her toes and pinching her fingers, not to mention sending gusts of onion-scented laughter into her face each time he made an error.

Alice was earnestly engaged in conversation with a sharp-featured lady on her other side, leaving Elizabeth to contemplate which of her three partners she disliked the most. Sir Jason sent her more than a few wheezes that seemed to concern his hunting pack in Leicestershire and the vast number of foxes on neighboring properties, which did not seem to reflect well on the excellence of his dogs or on the expertise of his hunting companions. Mr. Higgs told her of his last summer at Weymouth with his three children, ensuring her avoidance of that resort forever. Mr. Darrow explained in detail the attributes of his newest equipage, extolling its virtues to the point she thought he might be hoping she would buy it from him.

So far, it was a dull evening, size and elegance of the crowd notwithstanding. There was no lack, Elizabeth thought as she cast her eyes about the ballroom, of glittering jewels and elaborate gowns of the finest silks. No scarcity of gentlemen in waistcoats so garish that their valets must have suffered from indigestion at the sight. No shortage of stout matrons with bosoms overflowing their bodices. And a full crop of innocent maidens in virginal white, whether or not it flattered their complexions.

Elizabeth had not yet brought herself to choose gowns in bright colors. She had too long been in black. Tonight she wore a deep shade of green, a particularly fine background for her favorite jewelry, a rope of pearls Reginald gave her on the occasion of their first anniversary. She remembered thinking then how fortunate she was to have an arranged marriage turn out successfully.

If she had not been passionately enamored of Reginald, she had found him kind, thoughtful, and more than a good provider. Indeed, she could have asked for no more in a husband. Even after the changes in Reginald wrought by the years at Allward and the harangues he endured from his

mother, he was always considerate of her. He had
done the best thing a man could have done to
provide for his wife—left her a fortune to protect
her independence and her choices. For that she
would always honor his memory.

"Elizabeth!" Alice's voice broke into Elizabeth's
wandering thoughts. "Here he is!"

Elizabeth looked up, noting two men and a
woman coming their way through the throng. The
taller man with the light brown hair looked rather
familiar. In fact, as he neared, she recognized him
as Mr. Marlowe, the charming gentleman from
Lady Simpson's conservatory.

Alice leaned close and whispered in Elizabeth's
ear. "He is a most eligible gentleman, Lizzie—a widower for the last two years."

Elizabeth could not prevent a little gasp of surprise. Before she could completely recover her
composure, Alice gripped her elbow and they rose,
stepping forward to meet the trio. Elizabeth kept
her eyes lowered, for she feared if she met Mr. Marlowe's eyes, she would suddenly don the silliest of
bird-witted grins.

The pleasantries seemed to drag on for a long
time. She lifted her eyes for a moment when she
was formally introduced to Mr. Marlowe, just long
enough to catch his little wink. She took it for a signal that they would not reveal their prior meeting.

She smiled briefly at Sir James and Lady Powell
when she dipped her curtsies; otherwise, she con-
centrated on keeping her face as expressionless as
possible, hoping she appeared dignified and serene,
because inside she was feeling quite outrageously
fluttery.

Why? She had already spent a quarter hour in the
gentleman's presence, a rather unremarkable time
but mildly enjoyable. Yet the silliest thoughts had

flitted through her head, thoughts that centered on Mr. Marlowe's muscular yet trim look, on his wry humor, on his pleasant smile and the way his gray eyes caught the light, on his effortless recitation of the exotic plant species. His black evening dress was impeccably austere, his hair faultlessly cut.

Mr. Marlowe spoke softly. "Do you wish to stroll toward the refreshments, Mrs. Drayton? I suspect you might enjoy a glass of champagne."

She nodded. "Why, how prescient you are, Mr. Marlowe. You guessed my desire exactly."

He offered his elbow, and she felt entirely comfortable linking her hand through his arm. As they moved off, Elizabeth caught a glimpse of Alice's triumphantly beaming face.

Four

Once they were a few steps from the grinning faces of Alice and Lady Powell, Harry gave a little laugh. "Nicely done, Mrs. Drayton. I take it neither of us revealed that little chance meeting we had."

"Why, no. If I had mentioned it, I would have had no end of questions from my cousin."

"The same reaction would have been my fate if I had mentioned meeting you to Faith."

"Later on, we can both expect questioning worthy of the Inquisition, I suppose."

His laughter was a velvety rumble. "A devilish business, their conspiracy! Why is it our dear ones are so anxious to pair us up? Sometimes, it seems my sister is determined to introduce me to every lady in London."

At the champagne fountain, he filled a goblet and handed it to Elizabeth.

Elizabeth glanced behind her and spotted her cousin hovering not far away, ostensibly conversing with her friend Lady Daveny. But Elizabeth was not deceived for a moment.

"My cousin is keeping her eye on us, I believe."

"No doubt. My sister will be lurking too. She will be curious to see how we get along."

"Mr. Marlowe, you said you had an interest in botany. Do you have some flowers you particularly find easy to grow? Out of doors, I mean. Not under glass."

"Of course, there are many that flourish here. Are you having problems with your garden?"

"Oh, I have no garden at the moment, though I hope to have one before much time passes. I am currently living with my cousin and her husband."

He nodded with an encouraging smile.

"Please excuse me for going on so, but gardening seems like a pleasure I would enjoy. I shall have to start with the simplest of flowers, not that I equate your interest in the science of botany with my eventual puttering with a few blossoms."

"Why, Mrs. Drayton, what do you suppose drives our interest in the scientific side of botany if it is not the desire to create prettier blooms for ladies like you?"

"Now that is the silliest fiddle-faddle I have ever heard, Mr. Marlowe. I am surprised at you."

"Oh, how sad it is to be revealed so completely as a fraud. Now you see why my sister despairs of finding me a nice lady. She knows what a disaster I incur when I attempt to be charming."

"Now you are expecting me to protest and tell you how very enchanting I find your company, are you not?"

"How very astute a judge of character you are, Mrs. Drayton. You have revealed me to be both ridiculous and shallow. Now I shall endeavor to resurrect my reputation by proposing a new subject that has no unfortunate connotations." He gazed at the surrounding crowd of people then back at Elizabeth. "Let me see, should we discuss fashion, and if so, ladies' or men's choices of attire?"

"I'm afraid I know little of fashion. I follow my cousin's dictates, or rather I should say, the dictates of a modiste who must be amassing a fortune worthy of a peer from all the gowns she provides for Alice and her friends."

"Yes, the fashionable tailors are much the same. But if fashion is not a topic that interests you, perhaps you know some tastefully proper gossip."

"Does not the very definition of *gossip* remove it from the 'proper' category?"

He stopped and turned toward her, his eyes shining with humor. She met his laughter with her own.

"Mrs. Drayton, you could do me a great favor this evening. It would put me in the highest regard of my sister if I were to take you for a turn about the park some day. Would you be kind enough to favor me with a 'yes'?"

"Indeed. Such an engagement would make my cousin almost swoon with joy. So, how could we dare to disappoint them? Of course I will join you later in the week. But not Thursday. I have the firm promise of my cousin and her husband to accompany me to look at a few properties."

"So, that is why you will have a garden soon?"

"Yes, I am looking for a place to call my own."

"Perhaps I could come for you on Tuesday afternoon? I will be interested to hear how you plan to conduct your search. I have been meaning to engage in the hunt for a suitable property but have not yet found the time."

"So, you live with your sister?" Elizabeth blushed, realizing the impropriety of her question. "Forgive me. I do not mean to pry."

"That is not a problem, Mrs. Drayton. I have rooms not more than a short walk from here, in St. James. I spend a great deal of time at my sister's house in Mount Street, however, where I have a few experiments going in her glasshouse. It is a small one, nothing like Lady Simpson's grand display."

"Here you are!" Sir James, followed closely by

Lady Powell, Alice, and Blaine, patted Harry's shoulder.

Elizabeth felt Alice's eyes boring into her, just as the dowager's used to do, though for a different purpose entirely. A blush warmed her cheeks. This was exactly the situation she had vowed not to fall into, as she could practically see Alice considering where to hold the wedding breakfast.

Lady Powell took Elizabeth's hand. "Mr. and Mrs. Gifford have been kind enough to accept our invitation for dinner and to share our box at the opera next week Friday, Mrs. Drayton. I hope you will be able to join us."

With five sets of eyes focused on her face, Elizabeth hoped her skin was not flame red. "I would be pleased to come."

To her great distress, she was already looking forward to the evening.

When she entered Mrs. Welk's drawing room, Elizabeth felt as though she had been transported backward several thousand years. The space was crowded with artifacts and furniture that seemed to come from another world. Two enormous gilded sphinxes supported a thick marble slab beneath a mirror framed by gilded palm trees. Four columns were shaped from immense bare-chested statues like the temple figures she had seen in the engravings in *The Treasures of the Nile*. Winged creatures with the torsos of women and the paws of lions, jackal-headed gods of inky basalt, even an open-jawed crocodile with ruby-red eyes . . . Elizabeth hoped her shock was not evident in her face.

"Do you like it, my dear?" Mrs. Welk beamed at the croc and patted its head. "It is all the crack. Or so Mr. Garrison tells me."

"If Mr. Garrison says so, it is the premier design idea of the day," Alice whispered.

Mrs. Welk led them to a gray-haired lady, dressed in the height of fashion, who wore a dazzling array of jewels on her fingers. "Lady Robert, I wish to introduce you to my friends Mrs. Gifford and Mrs. Drayton."

All curtsies and niceties exchanged, Elizabeth sat on a blue silk sofa. She glanced down to see her feet next to the talons of an eagle clutching a glass ball at the base of the sofa leg. She accepted the offer of a teacup and set it down on a little table formed from the wing of a carved bird, an ibis or a crane, from the looks of it.

Mrs. Berwald leaned over and spoke in an undertone. "You will get used to it, my dear. It is a shock only the first time you see it. I hardly notice the claws and fangs anymore."

Elizabeth agreed, happy to decide immediately that whatever kind of house she eventually acquired, one style of furnishings she would not embrace was Egyptian.

Mrs. Welk, thin and rather bony, had corkscrew curls of iron gray under a lacy cap with dangling ribbons all tangled in her curls, and incongruously large feet. "Did you see the report that the Prince Regent held a Royal Hunt on Saturday?"

"Is he not a bit corpulent to be cavorting around the countryside after deer?" Mrs. Berwald, in contrast, had small and dainty feet, suitable for her little mincing steps, but was much thicker around the middle.

Lady Robert sat ramrod straight, though her hands never stopped moving, gesturing, fingering her brooch, tapping on the mosaic tabletop. "I can only say, I pity his poor horse."

Mrs. Berwald, her mouth in a perpetual smile,

shook her head. "We all know that the prince is not one for moderation."

"Particularly when it comes to his lady friends." Lady Robert reached over to rearrange the flowers in a small vase. "Nor, for that matter, do his brothers behave any better."

"Oh, my!" Mrs. Berwald's pale gold curls, their shine dimmed by streaks of silver, bobbed again. "It is said that the Duchess of York has gone back to Oatlands."

"I had heard from Maitland when I saw him last week that she was to quit town," Mrs. Welk said, gazing at the now-crooked flowers.

In moments, Lady Robert excused herself. "I have several more calls to make, my dears. I have enjoyed meeting you, Mrs. Drayton. You are a welcome addition to town."

Elizabeth rose and curtsied to Lady Robert. "Thank you, my lady." As far as she could remember, she had uttered no more than five words, but apparently they were satisfactory to Lady Robert.

When Mrs. Welk came back from seeing Lady Robert to the door, she perched beside Elizabeth on the sofa. "Now that Beatrice is gone, we can have that good coze. She is a dear soul, but a born meddler. Loves a good scandal. We have to be careful what we say around her."

Mrs. Berwald nodded. "Yes, we need to be discreet. But as for you, Mrs. Drayton, I think you have superior prospects. Do you not find her very pretty, Hattie? Though I do not think the dark green flatters her complexion."

"Very lovely, Georgie. I like the dark green."

Alice held up a hand. "Oh, please, remember she has green eyes."

Elizabeth did not bother to protest, feeling quite

strange at hearing herself dissected and examined like a specimen in a glass jar.

"Ah, the eyes, of course. But, Alice, she needs a better haircut, lighter on top, feathery along the sides."

Alice threw Elizabeth a look of amusement. "Did I not tell you so? You see, ladies, Elizabeth seems like a sweet and pliable female. But she has her stubborn strain as well."

Mrs. Berwald cocked her head to one side. "I say she would look good in gold and that new shade of blue. Her eyes would still be green."

Mrs. Welk took Elizabeth's hand in hers. "Haircut or not, my dear, tell us how you have been getting on."

"Alice has been kind. . . ."

"We want to know who you have met."

"And do not forget . . ."

"But first we have to hear about how she liked . . ."

While the two ladies argued about what Elizabeth should tell them, she and Alice rocked with silent laughter.

Mrs. Welk brought it to a halt. "If you have met Lord Concannon, be warned. His is an Irish title with little land and no income."

"Now, Hattie, he sports a fine wardrobe."

"Too fine by half. He has an impressive crest on his carriage, but he has to hire horses. So, beware of him. Not a good prospect for you, Mrs. Drayton."

Mrs. Berwald waved her hand in the air. "It does not have to be Concannon, but nevertheless, you must marry soon, my dear. You still have your beauty. When their looks begin to go, you cannot imagine what some women do to preserve them. All sorts of potions, rubbed into skin, then talk of paint and powder."

"Hair thins, wrinkles deepen, you begin to lose

your vision and scrunch up your eyes like an old hag. You go to fat or grow scrawny. . . ."

Elizabeth and Alice could not hold back their giggles.

Mrs. Berwald grinned too. "You two can laugh now, but when you start to age, the men look elsewhere. Every year there are more young ladies, many of them looking for a father rather than a husband. You start to age, and men, well, they . . ."

Mrs. Welk looked thoughtful. "But look at Prinny. He likes women a bit older."

"Well, Hattie, we both know there are some exceptions. I recall that young Mr. Foster who squired you. . . ."

Mrs. Welk's hand fluttered to her bosom. "Oh, Georgie, how can you bring up such ancient history? Be careful, or I will start telling tales about you. I believe you had quite a little fling with Sir Franklin, and he was young enough to . . ."

Mrs. Berwald tossed her curls and wiggled a little in her seat. "Well, actually, I had a much better time with his younger brother. . . ."

Elizabeth and Alice barely kept from falling into hysterics until they were on their way home. Then, they laughed until their sides ached and their faces felt numb.

When they returned to Brook Street, Blaine told Elizabeth he had a visitor while they were out. "Mr. Bowman came by, and I suspect he intended to ask me if you would entertain a proposal from him."

"What?"

"I was able to deflect his remarks, because I suspect you are not open to—"

"Thank you, Blaine. You are quite correct!"

* * *

Alice was in such a dither, Elizabeth was amazed that Alice did not jump out of her skin.

"This is only a little ride in the park. I have seen Hyde Park before, you know."

"But this is with Mr. Marlowe. How can you be so calm?"

In truth, Elizabeth was not calm, which frustrated her. She had never been a flirt, had found conversation difficult with most of the men Alice thought suitable. Why did this man affect her differently? With him, she talked and laughed as though she were an accomplished coquette.

Alice handed her the green-trimmed bonnet that matched her carriage dress. "Madame Kuony would love seeing you all decked out in this outfit."

"Mmmmm." Elizabeth did not intend to get into another discussion of her eye color. Alice evaluated every ell of fabric Elizabeth considered by the way its hue supposedly affected the color of her eyes.

"You must admit he is handsome."

"Yes, he is good looking." Too good looking, perhaps. Many women could be expected to notice and pursue him. But, she reminded herself, that was lucky, for she had no intention of contracting an alliance with Mr. Marlowe or anybody else.

When Elizabeth settled the bonnet on her head, Alice brushed her hands away and tied a big bow at her cheek.

"There. You look perfect. He will not be able to resist you. I predict a quick settlement."

"Nonsense. Why do you think he wants another wife?"

"All men need wives to keep their lives organized and their households running smoothly."

Elizabeth shook her head. "Sounds like they would be better off with a good valet and an efficient housekeeper."

Alice rolled her eyes and sighed. "You are impossible."

When Mr. Marlowe arrived, Alice slipped away. Instead of engaging him in conversation, she disappeared with a quick wave.

"I have Faith's barouche as it is such a pleasant afternoon."

Elizabeth nodded and accepted his arm as they left the house.

Until they reached the park, their conversation was unexceptionable as were the sunshine, the horses, and the traffic they passed. Once the horses were trotting on the well-raked gravel of the Hyde Park paths, he brought up the subject of houses.

"Now, I would like to hear about your quest for a house, Mrs. Drayton."

"I am afraid I hardly know how to go about it. I asked Mr. Lytton, my man-of-business, to make a list of a few available properties. That is how I plan to begin."

"Much more efficient than just driving around and asking. I admit I have given it little thought."

"I know I may be unusual to want a house of my own. Alice thinks I am cabbage-headed to consider living alone."

"Perhaps she is worried about you."

"That might be part of it. But primarily, she thinks I should marry again."

"And that idea does not appeal to you?"

"Definitely not."

"Your feelings are not unlike my own. Faith thinks I should take a second wife, but I do not agree."

For a moment, Elizabeth paused. She wondered if this was a proper subject for them. But why not? Who would understand better than another who had lost a spouse? "But I take it your sister does not believe you know your own mind on the subject?"

"She thinks she knows best."

Elizabeth gave a trill of laughter. "As does Alice. I wonder what makes them so sure of their opinions?"

"My sister and her husband rub along quite well. I cannot claim that she is reflecting the old adage that misery loves company."

"The same is true of Alice and Blaine. She believes in the power of love."

He turned to look at her. "And you do not?"

"I fear I am not qualified to . . . or perhaps I should . . ." Elizabeth paused. Her marriage to Reginald gave her very limited knowledge of love.

Mr. Marlowe glanced at her, then looked back to the team. "I realize that is a difficult question. Love is one of those subjects beyond definition, I suppose."

"Yes, perhaps love is to be desired but not easily found."

"And so, rather than contract a marriage without love, of one kind or another, you choose to live alone?"

"Yes, I do. My cousin thinks I will be lonely, but to me, the right to follow my own whims sounds delicious. I realize that is shallow and selfish."

"I do not agree with that characterization. If one has spent a great deal of time catering to others' needs, it is perfectly understandable that one wishes to have a bit of autonomy."

"Thank you for being so perceptive. Alice says I dare not even suggest to others that I wish to be free and independent. They will think me eccentric, though I really would not mind if they did. But while I am so obliged to Alice and Blaine, I do not want to embarrass them."

"Your consideration for their view is admirable, but if they are only providing you a place to live . . ."

"Oh, they have done much more than that. You see, they came up to Yorkshire and once they were there, my husband's mother could hardly keep me from leaving. But if they had not come, I would probably still be there. I owe them everything."

"But not forever."

"True. I have even convinced them to look at some houses with me tomorrow."

"You have progressed further than I have. I have only wished I could find a house."

They reached an unoccupied stretch of the path, and he urged the horses to a faster pace.

"Well, Mrs. Drayton, I think the gentlemen of London will have their work cut out for them if they are to convince you to give up your unwed status for one of them. But you must know that with your many charms, particularly those lovely green eyes, you will be in constant demand whether you are living at Alice's house or in a cottage in Reading. They will find you, indeed they will."

Elizabeth groaned inwardly and shook her head.

He laughed. "You do not agree?"

"That is not it. I argued with Alice when she said my eyes were green. Now you are supporting her position."

He took the reins in one hand and turned her chin toward him with the other. "Green. Just like a purring cat, my dear. You cannot escape a fact."

"Oh my, now I am in the suds!" She broke into laughter again. "When Alice requests a report on our conversation, shall I have to say you called me a feline?"

"Feline, meaning graceful, lithe, and lovely? Why not?"

Her words caught in her throat. Of all the compliments she had received in the past few weeks, why did this one suddenly tie her tongue?

He slowed the horses to a walk as they came upon

a cluster of carriages. She waved and nodded to several acquaintances.

Elizabeth was relieved to have a change of topic. "The lady in that last vehicle is Lady Adeline Lynden, a connection of Alice's."

"Ah, yes. I believe my sister, Faith, mentioned her. Thinks she is Mary, Queen of Scots?"

"Not exactly, but Mary is her favorite topic of conversation. In fact, her only topic. But she is a kind-hearted soul, and though she forgets with whom she is speaking, she remembers an amazing variety of facts about the doomed queen. For example, I had forgotten Mary stayed with Bess of Hardwick."

The park paths had grown crowded with equipages turned out for the fashionable daily parade.

Mr. Marlowe tipped his hat to numerous vehicles, and he and Elizabeth stopped to exchange pleasantries with several. Sir Ennis, driving a high-perched phaeton with bright yellow wheels, waved to Elizabeth while his passengers, a buxom woman in a bonnet of cerise and a young lady in pale yellow gestured to Mr. Marlowe.

"A lovely day in the park, Mrs. Drayton. I say, it is a lovely day," said Sir Ennis.

"Oh, Mr. Marlowe, Prudence has learned a new poem, practically in your honor—"

Elizabeth jumped as the carriage suddenly lurched forward.

Mr. Marlowe pretended to fiddle with the reins. "Whoa, there. So very nice to see you," he called as they moved on.

When they were well past the phaeton, Elizabeth whispered to him. "For shame, Mr. Marlowe."

"I hope these poor horses forgive me. But that was Mrs. Fitzmaurice-Smythe and her poor daughter. I have had too many narrow escapes at that woman's hands. I wish to discourage her if at all possible."

"Well, riding with Sir Ennis would discourage me. He says everything twice, everything twice."

Mr. Marlowe laughed. "I know. I know."

"Perhaps they are meant for each other."

"Tell me, Mrs. Drayton, does it make sense to you for a woman like Mrs. Fitzmaurice-Smythe to want a husband who is my age for her eighteen-year-old daughter?"

"Many families look to older men for their daughters. My husband was thirty-six, precisely twice my age when we wed."

"So, it was an arranged marriage?"

"More or less. My father brought Reginald to the house several times. Then they told me our betrothal agreement was being drawn up, and was I not a lucky female?"

"So, that is how it is done. Some sort of relic from the Middle Ages, in my opinion."

"If my mother had been alive, perhaps it would have been different. Father thought he was doing the right thing in finding me a good provider. And I was not unhappy. I did not resist. But my views were never sought."

"Well, Mrs. Fitzmaurice-Smythe was quite a bit sneakier. A few weeks ago, she tried to close me up in Lord Norwell's library with her mule-faced daughter. Apparently, she thought if I was caught alone with the chit, I would have to offer for her."

"What? She tried to trap you?"

"That was only the closest call. Luckily, I realized her intent and simply left the room."

"No wonder there are so many unhappy marriages."

"Mrs. Drayton, your perception is splendid!"

Five

"The carriage will be waiting for us at eleven."
Elizabeth stood at the foot of Alice's bed, watching
her cousin pull the covers over her head. "That
gives you one hour, dearest."

Alice groaned; her words were muffled. "Why so
early?"

"Because we have five houses to see, and I do not
want to miss any of them."

The covers shook. "Lizzie, please. We can go
later, after noon."

"Alice! You promised. I will send your maid."

Elizabeth did not wait for further argument but
headed downstairs, called the maid, and sat at the little writing desk in the morning room. Spread before
her were the sheets sent by her man-of-business describing each of the houses. She had read them so
many times she had almost memorized the details,
and she felt a little frisson of anticipation. Soon she
would actually see the houses and be on her way to
fulfilling her ambition.

In just half an hour, before Elizabeth had
completed her hundredth reading, Alice came
downstairs.

"Elizabeth, please come have a cup of tea while I
eat a bite. After that late supper last night, I thought
I might never eat again. But strangely enough, I am
ravenous this morning."

Elizabeth followed her into the breakfast room and took a chair across the table. When they were served, she watched Alice spread jam on a triangle of toast.

"Do you know I have never had a house of my own?"

Alice looked up in surprise. "Is that so? What do you mean?"

"I left Papa's to marry Reginald, and he already had a house. It was completely furnished, and I do not recall making more than the tiniest changes. Then we went to live at Allward. The only thing I ever changed there was the wall color. I asked to have our suite of rooms painted, covering the dark brown with an ivory shade. The dowager was distraught, partly because it took three coats."

Alice finished her first piece of toast and reached for another. "If you want only to furnish your room in our house, I will give you a free hand. And do up the sitting room again if you wish. Use five coats of paint!"

"Oh, Alice, how very sweet of you. But I cannot impose on you forever. And I do have the desire to . . ."

"I suppose I can see your view, though I think you are wrong. Will you not be lonely?"

"Just the thought of the dowager's constant observation or those awful improving tracts we read together—do not think for a moment that I will be lonely after years of that kind of companionship."

Blaine leaned around the corner of the doorway. "Shall I request the carriage to be here in a quarter hour?"

Elizabeth looked around with a smile. "I will be ready."

Alice's response was less enthusiastic. "I, too, will be ready, Blaine. But I can only repeat, darling cousin Lizzie, that I think you would be happier with a nice, comfortable husband, someone who appreciates you for yourself, not only for your fat purse."

Elizabeth's jaw tightened, but she kept herself from frowning. Alice meant well. "The worst thing would be to meet a man who is only after my money. I cannot imagine anything more lowering." Unless it was the way she had been married off to Reginald without anyone considering her thoughts on the matter.

"Oh, it might not be so bad. There are many wonderful men who do not have a handsome income. Some might be important in the government. Lizzie, you would make a good political hostess. And what is the use of having money if it does not make you happy?"

"I intend to be happy in my own house." Happy in a way she had never known but had always yearned for—happy on her own terms with no one dictating to her.

"Without a man in your life? You don't want to move into a big house all by yourself."

"I'll have servants." Elizabeth stood. "I need to get my bonnet."

"Wait a minute"—Alice grabbed her hand—"You know what I mean. Even as a widow, you cannot go about freely. You need a husband to afford you total freedom. The freedom to do *nothing* is what you are going to have, my dear."

Elizabeth pulled away. "Nonsense! Do not tell me that, Alice. There are widows who are quite active in ton events."

"But they are much, much older. Or quite notorious. Certainly you do not want to acquire a shady reputation!"

"Of course not. The very thought is ridiculous."

"Then take my advice and find yourself an agreeable husband. Mr. Marlowe would be the ideal match for you." Alice joined Elizabeth in climbing the stairs to seek out their wraps.

No one, Elizabeth silently vowed again, would talk her out of finding her own house. And no one would talk her into taking on another marriage just to adhere to ridiculous edicts of fashionable Society. She and Mr. Marlowe quite agreed on that subject.

When she came down, Elizabeth was surprised to see Sir Howell Newby standing on the black and white marble tiles of the foyer. He was an earnest fellow with whom she had danced at a ball last week, a member of one of Blaine's clubs. Above a rather long nose, he had close-set dark eyes and reminded her of a remarkably ugly portrait of Charles II. But without the monarch's reputed charm.

"Good morning, Sir Howell. Are you here looking for Mr. Gifford?"

"Good day, Mrs. Drayton." He bowed and noisily cleared his throat. "No, I am . . . well, yes . . . that is, Blaine told me about your . . . your inspection of houses this morning. I have . . . you see, I will be glad to accompany you . . . I am something of an expert . . . that is, I know . . . a great deal . . ."

Blaine's entry mercifully cut short Sir Howell's laborious statement. "Sir Howell, glad you could join us. We will be going as soon as Mrs. Gifford is ready."

Elizabeth's heart fell, her eagerness to be underway no longer tempting her to run upstairs and drag Alice from her room. Sir Howell's company was most unwelcome indeed, probably just another voice trying to compel her to abandon her idea of finding a house.

"I am coming," Alice called from above.

Naturally she was ready, now that Elizabeth had to think of a way to circumvent Sir Howell's companionship.

In the next few moments, as she realized Alice and Blaine had no objection to Sir Howell's presence, indeed seemed to welcome it, Elizabeth tried to break into the conversation to protest. But she could not think of a single objection that did not seem extremely rude.

Alice was oblivious to her distress, chattering in her usual manner. "Blaine says Sir Howell is well versed in all the problems of houses, being something of an architect himself."

Elizabeth's thoughts took a further dive into dejection. Next thing he would want to do was design a house for her himself.

His very appearance made her want to send him away, for he wore the striped satin waistcoat of a confirmed dandy. The brass buttons on his bright blue coat were as large as saucers.

"But I am sure you have many more important things to do with your day, Sir Howell. I could not bear to impose upon you like this."

"Why no, Mrs. Drayton, my dear . . . that is, I am perfectly willing . . . you might even say I am eager . . . that is, it is my pleasure." He took her hand in his damp palm and squeezed it.

Elizabeth withdrew her hand and wished she had a basin of water and some soap with which to wash.

"The carriage is here." Blaine's announcement was tantamount to an order as he was most particular about preventing his horses from standing more than a moment.

Elizabeth, her mood altered in the last quarter hour from exhilarated to glum, tried not to grimace as she accepted Sir Howell's help into the carriage.

Despite Sir Howell's presence, Elizabeth's excitement returned as the carriage headed out of Mayfair. At the first of the houses, a newly built terrace just a short distance away, she knew before she entered that it was not what she wanted. There was only a tiny yard and houses pressed close to it on both sides. However, for the sake of comparison, she led the way up three stone steps to the entrance.

A footman bade them enter and showed them the ground floor dining room and study. Both had furniture pushed into the middle and covered with dust sheets. Elizabeth wondered how she could judge the size of a room when the furnishings were out of place.

Blaine wandered into the corridor. "The staircase is handsome. I like the curving metal banister, quite fashionable in a newer house."

Elizabeth and Alice followed him. One glance and Elizabeth knew she far preferred the mellow shine of well-waxed wooden railings, but she kept her opinion to herself. The style of a staircase would not be the determining factor in her choice.

Sir Howell pointed to the fireplaces. "Good modern fittings there. That is a favorable sign."

The drawing rooms on the first floor had tall windows, with a light and airy atmosphere, but again Elizabeth wondered how large the space would be if the chairs and sofas were distributed around the room instead of bunched together and covered over. In the bedrooms above, the walls wore the latest in patterned paper, but there was no furniture at all.

After thanking the footman, the party got back into the carriage.

"What did you think?" Blaine asked.

Sir Howell shrugged. "Not the very best construction in these new terraces . . . that is to say, barely adequate. Some shortcuts perhaps, but nothing serious."

"I found it hard to judge the house," Elizabeth

said. "But I really prefer something a bit farther out of town with a little more room for a garden."

Alice seemed more impressed. "I thought it was handsome and very modern. Who knows, Blaine, we might find something more suitable for ourselves. I have always thought the Brook Street house a bit too small for the kind of parties I like to give."

Elizabeth watched Blaine's reaction, hoping he would not take offense. He only smiled indulgently.

"Whatever makes you happy, my pet."

Alice grimaced. "Why, you cad, to tease me so! Just a sennight ago, you said you never wanted to change residences again."

He laughed out loud. "I did, indeed. But if you promise, my dear, to supervise all the packing and arrangement of the new dwelling, I suppose I might reconsider."

"You see?" Alice turned to Sir Howell. "He is only bamming me. He knows I would never be able to undertake such a project alone."

"Perhaps you can practice by helping me." Elizabeth nodded to Blaine. "Though I have little to move. Only a few things in storage from Reginald's London house."

Alice's grin widened. "Then we shall have a busy time visiting the warehouses. Perhaps we should also do a bit of refurnishing, my dear?"

Blaine's response was a little laugh.

Alice ignored his lack of enthusiasm. "I think I might enjoy helping you, Lizzie. If, that is, you go through with your plan. I still believe you should form an alliance with a suitable man and let him do the difficult bits."

Sir Howell cleared his throat nosily.

Elizabeth decided to hold her tongue. Alice obviously was in a mischievous mood.

Their arrival at the second place on her list

placed Elizabeth in another difficult conversation with Sir Howell.

"Mrs. Drayton," he began ponderously. "I do believe you should . . . that is, I would recommend, if you would be so kind . . . Well, here we are."

The house was one of a group of six new houses in a decorative cottage ornée style, all grouped around a green. Each property had a rear garden and shared the use of the decorative central lawn and its attractive fountain.

To Elizabeth, the area had a contrived look, just a little too perfect, too artificial.

The inside was no better, completely empty and echoing. "I realize things would look different if the furnishings were in place, but it does not feel warm to me. Something is missing."

Alice agreed. "Perhaps it is just too new."

The main bedchamber seemed dark, tucked up under a roof designed to look like rural thatching, with very small, diamond-paned windows as though it dated from Tudor times.

Sir Howell had little that was positive to say. "I would say the foundations are sound, but again, new construction is often put up too quickly, with . . . with too little attention to quality."

When they were again on their way, Elizabeth sighed deeply. "I love houses that have elements dating from many centuries, but that one definitely did not look genuine."

Blaine nodded. "I agree. That was not the place for you."

The next house was no closer to her dreams than the previous two had been, far too small for her taste. Sir Howell pointed out some broken stonework and questioned the reliability of the flashing.

The fourth property was far too big, an estate really, without the home farm, but with many acres of empty pasture.

Elizabeth laughed as they toured the outbuildings. "Unless I decide to raise sheep and keep a dozen horses, I cannot imagine what I would do with all this."

Both Alice and Blaine agreed.

Sir Howell appeared around the corner of the house. "I can recommend this . . . foundations are sound and the cellars are dry . . . must check the cellars, my dear . . . Damp bodes ill for the humors in the house."

Finding the fifth house brought them nearer the Thames, but the view was mostly blocked by tall trees that grew on a neighboring property.

When the party returned to Mayfair, they dropped Sir Howell in St. James Street.

Elizabeth gave him her sweetest smile. "You have my profound thanks, Sir Howell. You taught me a great deal today, things I never would have considered."

"My pleasure . . . that is, I consider it an honor . . . always glad to be of service . . ." He lifted a hand as the carriage rolled off.

"He may look like a dandy, but he knows of what he speaks," Blaine said.

Elizabeth rested her head on the squabs. "I agree. I was quite apprehensive when he arrived this morning, but I believe his advice is sound."

Blaine stretched out his legs. "Please explain, Elizabeth, why you want to look farther from town. What do you want in a house?"

Before she answered, Alice raised more questions. "Is the house more important than having neighbors? You would have to make a whole set of new friends."

"Yes, and you are thinking I am not very good

with new acquaintances. I am still too shy, and I will be lonely."

Alice took her hand. "Exactly. I can understand a bit about you wanting to have your own house. But you are a young woman. You need to have a husband and children, not bury yourself in an obscure corner and read novels all alone."

Blaine still looked skeptical. "I do not understand why you are not looking in Mayfair or one of the squares just to the north."

"I suppose I am a rural girl at heart."

Alice exhaled noisily. "Not I. I far prefer to be in town with all the comforts."

Blaine patted her hand. "My pet, you probably would not even ride in the park if it were not a fashionable activity."

As they neared Brook Street, Elizabeth spoke softly, half to herself. "I was hoping to like at least one of the houses, but at least I now have some standards for comparison."

"Why you would want to be anywhere but right here is a mystery to me!" Alice gathered her shawl and prepared to climb out of the carriage. "As for now, I think I shall indulge in a restful lie-down."

Elizabeth followed Alice upstairs and tossed her reticule on her bed. What would Mr. Marlowe have thought of the estate property? Perhaps it would be just what he was looking for, and as she opened her writing desk, she ran over the estate's attributes to fix them in her mind. She dipped her pen to begin a more specific list of her requirements to send to Mr. Lytton. But halfway through the first sentence, she found herself lost in thoughts about yesterday's outing with Mr. Marlowe.

You are too tired, she told herself sternly.

* * *

The next evening, as she prepared for the musicale, Elizabeth took particular care with her gown and hair. Though she wondered just why this was, in her heart she knew she was thinking about encountering Mr. Marlowe again. In fact, she was looking forward to seeing him and hoped he would be in attendance. She wanted to tell him about that house with all the land.

But much later, as the hour neared midnight, she realized he was not coming and she felt very downcast, though she was garnering a considerable amount of attention from the gentlemen on hand, more than she wished for.

Just as she was hoping to sit down and avoid dancing the next set, Alice hastened up with another gentleman, the third of the evening. "Elizabeth, look who I found! Sir Ennis has just arrived."

The portly fellow bowed deeply. "Good evening, Mrs. Drayton. Good evening. I have just come from the theater. Come from the theater, indeed."

Elizabeth winced. She had met Sir Ennis several times and a more self-important fellow she could not imagine, a man of limitless arrogance made more serious because of his irksome habit of repeating everything. But she smiled in what she hoped was a welcoming way.

"Good evening to you, Sir Ennis."

"I hope you are well. Hope you are well." He wore a jacket of jade green brocade with an immense starched neckcloth that threatened to throttle him.

Alice had quickly melted away into the crowd.

"Would you like to take a seat, Sir Ennis? I am in need of a little breather."

He led the way to the chairs. "It is a lively set. A very lively set."

When she was seated, he lowered himself into a

chair with a flourish that belied his bulk. "I am most honored to sit with you."

He made a little pause, and Elizabeth mouthed the words along with him. "Honored to sit with you."

The thought of spending more than five minutes in his company was impossible. Impossible. Even in her head, she was doing it too. Doing it . . .

She shivered her shoulders to shake off the galling pattern.

"Perhaps I could get you a wrap."

She cringed at his next words.

"Get you a wrap."

"No, thank you," she said, clamping her mouth shut before she said it again. Why did Mr. Marlowe not appear? He would be most welcome tonight. Instead, she repeated her words. "No, thank you, Sir Ennis. I think I shall withdraw for a few moments."

Alice followed her to the ladies' retiring room where they found themselves alone other than the maid.

Alice was ecstatic. "Lord Charles Bonamy is the heir to the Earl of Upton. You had two full sets with him, did you not? And he took you in to dinner?"

"He is a mere baby, no more than twenty-two, much too young for me. Even if I were interested in contracting an alliance, which you know I am not, I would think him much too young."

"He seems quite struck by you, Elizabeth."

"I am definitely not interested in mothering a young man who needs a few years of experience before he is likely to fall truly in love. What would his parents think of him marrying an older woman, a widow?"

"I cannot imagine they would object. Someday he will inherit the earldom and its considerable income."

"He needs more years on the town, as they say. Or a grand tour. He certainly does not need me."

"Elizabeth, you have no idea how attractive you are. How your beauty shines. How appealing your quiet ways and gentleness are. You are not only amiable, you are rich. I have respected your wishes and told no one of your fortune, but information like that somehow gets around."

"But who would tell?"

"You have spoken with a man-of-business, solicitors, house agents—they might not spend much time in ton ballrooms, but they talk elsewhere and the word spreads."

"Are you certain you have said nothing?"

"Not a word." Alice lowered her voice to a murmur. "Think of the servants. They talk to one another. They meet in the market or wait for us at the theater. The coachmen talk, the footmen, even butlers have been known to commit an occasional *faux pas.*"

Elizabeth frowned at her image in the looking glass. She did not care to be pursued by men who needed money, whether it was because they had little after gambling it away or because they were spending beyond their resources. How could she trust anyone?

Certainly not Mr. Raft, whose words had been so polite while his eyes were pasted on her bosom and who tried to maneuver her so that her neckline gaped and improved his view. Too bad she had not tucked a crimson kerchief down her bosom to give him a real shock.

Elizabeth yearned to crawl into bed when she finally sent her maid away. "I shall see you in the morning, Lolly."

The maid curtsied and left, probably off to flirt with one of the footmen below stairs. An innocent flirtation . . . It sounded harmless. But it seemed Elizabeth would never know what it meant to enjoy the company of a gentleman who was not already predisposed to consider her a prospective match, accompanied as she was by a considerable fortune. Rumors of her wealth were no doubt responsible for her growing popularity with the ton, as insignificant as that was in the great scheme of things.

She climbed into bed and turned down the lamp. Only Mr. Marlowe seemed interested in her as a person, not a bank account with a pretty face. Most certainly, he did not intend to marry. He had said so emphatically.

Not that it mattered. Once she had her house, she would not need to go out at all if she . . . Oh, how ungrateful she sounded. Alice was terribly kind and enjoyed every moment of it, a born matchmaker.

Whatever her motive, Alice was doing what she thought best for Elizabeth. But it was not what Elizabeth wanted. Now, she who had once been so timid was determined to assert her independence. Nothing was going to come in the way of that.

She tucked the covers around herself. She tried to recall Reginald's face but could not form the image in her mind. Had she been a good wife to him? As she recalled, most of the time he hardly noticed she was there.

As the second son of an earl, Reginald had chosen to make his way in the world by undertaking the building of a fortune for himself. Very quietly he found schemes for building canals, developing cotton mills, and constructing turnpikes and found other investments in shipping, not to mention partnerships abroad. He rarely shared information about his activities with her, and she rarely asked him any questions.

Elizabeth wondered how she had filled her days in those first few years of marriage. She had hoped for a child, of course, but her hopes were disappointed month after month. Then their life had changed with Reginald's return to Allward and his assumption of the duties of manager of all the estate's matters and businesses. As the years in Yorkshire passed, he told Elizabeth only that he kept his former interests intact and worked on them by mail and on occasional trips to London.

Now she alone would reap the benefits of Reginald's talents. She would find a home of her own, a place to reflect her own tastes and no one else's. It would be a place of many windows and much light, of colorful walls and comfortable, plush furniture. Her own boudoir would be full of satins and laces in pale pinks and sky blues. Or perhaps lemon yellows and spring greens. She looked forward to choosing the fabrics and designs herself. . . .

Six

Harry arrived at his sister's residence early enough to check his seedlings before Mrs. Drayton and her cousins arrived. Though he looked carefully at each tiny plant, he found his mind more occupied with thoughts of what Mrs. Drayton might be wearing than with the readiness of his project for transplantation. *You are falling much too much under the influence of your sister.*

Through no fault of her own, Mrs. Drayton seemed to be invading his brain quite frequently, it seemed. Last evening at Sir Joseph's house, he needed to give himself a mental kick several times to maintain his attention on the conversation.

As much as he had longed to return to South America, he wondered how he would adapt to life aboard a ship again. What had been a great adventure when he was only eighteen might be, this time, years of uncomfortable and often tedious imprisonment in a cramped, smelly, and even dangerous vessel.

Here was a disturbing paradox. Now that his fellow botany enthusiasts were putting the voyage together, he had met a lady whose company he quite enjoyed. Yet, he yearned to be back in the forests and jungles, searching for new species, particularly of his admired bromeliads. The specimens he had obtained were now well established at Kew,

and even here at Faith's there were four tall,
healthy stalks.

He walked over to the *Guzmania lingulata,* probably his favorite among the exotic plants. Unlike its
close relative, the pineapple, this bromeliad was sig-
nificant mainly for its pretty color and unique shape.

"Harry!" Faith tapped at the glass door. "Come
out of there right away. Our guests are driving up."
She hurried off without waiting for him.

Faith's call caused his thoughts to return again to
Mrs. Drayton. Unconsciously he checked to see if
his cravat had collapsed in the dampness, but luckily he had not been inside the conservatory long
enough to wilt it.

Biting the inside of his lip to prevent too wide a
smile, he closed the conservatory door behind him
and hastened toward the anteroom, where he stood
watching the three guests below.

The footman lifted Elizabeth's cloak from her
shoulders. Harry felt a surge of interest in what she
might be wearing, another dark gown no doubt, as
she seemed to keep close to the shades of her recent mourning.

As she stepped into the light of the staircase, he
felt his breath catch in his throat. Before he noticed
the color of her gown, his eyes were captured by
its low neckline, or rather, by the expanse of creamy
skin above it. By Society's standards, it was quite
modest, but in comparison with what she had previously worn, it was a distinct improvement.

Harry knew nothing of fashion, only that her
gown was the color of deep claret, made of silk
that looked almost black except where the direct
light hit it and showed the richness of fine wine
held up before a candle. The sleeves of her
gown—well, there were hardly any sleeves, leaving her shoulders bare and a stretch of her upper

arms equally unclothed to the top of her long
gloves. In her light hair, Elizabeth wore a circlet
of flowers, all made of the same shimmering
shade. Whenever she moved, the fabric changed,
drawing his eye, glimmering, teasing. What was
more intriguing—the swell of her breasts, the velvet of her arms, or the glimmer of her gown?
Whichever it was, Harry found himself mesmerized by her beauty.

Elizabeth kept her eyes lowered as she stepped
into Lady Powell's handsome townhouse. She had
the feeling she might break into an unbecoming
grin when she saw Mr. Marlowe again—and blush
deeply for everyone to see. Certainly, Alice would
not miss her flushed cheeks and would later tease
her mercilessly. She could never explain to Alice
her desire for independence if she reddened like a
schoolgirl every time she encountered Mr. Marlowe. Inside, Elizabeth knew it was only that he was
so very kind, so nice to her. He was a very pleasant
gentleman; that was all. Just that afternoon, Alice
had declared him by far the best of the lot and had
told Elizabeth to grab him. If Elizabeth could not
demonstrate her indifference to him tonight, Alice
would be after her to order wedding clothes.

They climbed a curving staircase adorned with
marble statues in familiar poses. Elizabeth raised
her eyes only to acknowledge the greetings of her
host and hostess and to steal a glimpse of the
room's decor. Intense yellows dominated the room.
Handsome sofas were covered in brocade the shade
of the summer's sunniest marigolds. On the carpet,
medallions of gold and yellow lay on a background
of black and white, complementing the stunning
carved ebony chairs and tables. Lady Powell wore a

gown obviously chosen to complement her chestnut hair and to match the brilliant yellow of her
drawing room.

The painting over the fireplace showed a couple
in the garb of sixty years ago. A mother held a
chubby child while a small boy of about three stood
beside his father.

Noticing her guests' interest, Lady Powell explained. "That is our grandfather, Baron Tracey,
with our uncle, and our grandmother holding our
father, Justin Marlowe, barely ten months old when
they were painted in the 1760s. Our uncle, the sixth
Baron Tracey, has a later version of the family.
Uncle always thought this canvas made him much
too pretty, like a little girl. He claims he never had
such curls. Today, he has only a fringe of hair."

She took a pair of miniatures from the shelf and
handed them to Alice who admired them and
passed them along to Elizabeth. "These are my
boys, both away at school now. Seth, the youngest,
is at Eton, and Gerald is at Cambridge, just beginning King's College. I miss them terribly."

Elizabeth felt a stronger tie to Lady Powell. "My
nephew is going to Eton soon, I hope."

"I am sure he will thrive there." Lady Powell's
smile extended to her vivid blue eyes. "There is a
portrait of the boys downstairs in the dining room.
We had it painted last year, before Seth was off to
school."

They were seated in the drawing room before
Elizabeth allowed herself to look in Mr. Marlowe's
direction. He smiled at her and she nodded to him,
quickly redirecting her gaze. Like his brother-in-
law, Harry was dressed quietly in a coat of deepest
midnight blue over an ivory waistcoat. He wore no
fobs or stickpins in his cravat, only a signet ring.

She suppressed her desire to start talking

immediately about the houses, for she was eager to tell him about what she had seen. But to be so forward seemed inappropriate.

In mere moments, however, Sir James escorted Blaine to the library to see an item in the Edinburgh newspapers, and Faith, linking her arm through Alice's, led her to the morning room on some pretext.

Abruptly, Elizabeth and Mr. Marlowe were alone.

He walked to the fireplace and stirred the coals. "I assume their actions are as transparent to you as they are to me."

Elizabeth kept herself from a nervous giggle. "I did not think they would be quite so obvious as to leave us alone within five minutes."

"No doubt they conferred in advance on the timing of our *tête à tête,* the dinner, and the theater. As conspirators, they are appallingly obvious."

Mr. Marlowe crossed the room and sat in a black and gilt chair near hers. "I should like to hear about your house-hunting venture. How was it?"

"Disappointing in that I found nothing to my liking, but also enlightening because I learned more about what I need to ask for."

"Do you mean size and number of rooms or areas of town?"

"All of those things, but now I can eliminate a terrace house, for example. And I want to be away from the bustle and noise, perhaps in a village nearby."

"So, you would leave London?"

"I will tell you a secret that would greatly distress my cousin. The farther from London we went, the more attraction I felt for the houses."

"When you said you wanted a garden, you meant more than a plot between the house and the mews?"

"Yes, indeed. I saw a property that might interest

you, Mr. Marlowe. It was a much larger property than I want. In Twickenham, a nice house with many outbuildings, several pastures, and plenty of space for a conservatory and special gardens." She took a slip of paper from her reticule and handed it to him. "You need only apply to the caretaker, and he will show you around."

"But you found nothing that suited you?"

"No, I have written to my man about further searches, and I expect to look around again in a few days. Perhaps one of them will be the house of my dreams."

"What are your dreams, Mrs. Drayton?"

"I see a house full of light, perhaps on a hill, with a view of the Thames, near enough to central London that I can travel back and forth in a reasonable amount of time, but far enough to be rural in feeling."

"You have been to the gardens at Kew. Did you look in that area?"

"No, I did not go quite that far."

"Well, you might like the area around Richmond—a charming topography and a lively town with its own character. Not precisely a little rural village, but a place where there is theater and shopping and many well-connected people around."

"I know Richmond only as the site of a ruined palace of the Tudors."

"The village has considerable charm."

"One of the houses suggested to me is not far from there. I think the place is called Putney."

"I look forward to hearing more about your search."

"I have to get Alice and Blaine to take me again. Or perhaps hire a companion . . ."

Just as the others joined them, the butler

announced dinner, causing Elizabeth and Mr. Marlowe to exchange smiles.

When they arrived at the opera house, Mr. Marlowe took Elizabeth's cloak. His cool hand grazed the bare skin of her upper arm, leaving a tingly spot that she was sure glowed like firelit ice. Alice sat beside her, discussing menus with Lady Powell. Elizabeth could not concentrate on either the discussion of food or on the singer who opened the bill.

Harry found himself alone with Mrs. Drayton again. At the end of the first act, the four conspirators quickly left the box and probably were guarding the door, as no one entered, despite the fact that several ladies had waved their fans at him and Mrs. Drayton had been the focus of attention from several gentlemen in nearby boxes.

Elizabeth glanced around at the empty chairs, a look of surprise on her face. "Those connivers have snared us again, it seems."

"Snared? I hope you do not feel uncomfortable here, Mrs. Drayton."

"Oh no, that is not what I meant at all. I just find it amazing that our relations have left us alone once more."

"But this time in full view of several hundred people."

"Yes, it is an amazing sight. There is a lady over there who is wearing a turban so high that no one behind her will be able to see the stage."

"I think some husbands encourage their wives to wear elaborate headpieces. Then they can sit behind the ladies and be shielded from discovery while they nap through the performance."

"Aha! Now I see the reasoning."

He surveyed the boxes across the theater. "I would not put it past Faith to run around to the other side and sneak into an opposite box to watch us. Would not surprise me to know she had a spy-glass secreted in her reticule."

"Unless Alice has brought hers along." Elizabeth lowered her voice to a whisper. "Or perhaps Alice is listening from the next box. Nothing they do will surprise me."

"I assure you, we shall not be overheard, even if Faith has her ear pressed to the door. Now, as long as we are alone here, as alone as we can be with the potential for a thousand eyes to be trained on every little movement we make, we can talk about virtually anything. Anything, that is, that does not cause one of us to break into gales of loud laughter or burst into tears."

Elizabeth glanced around the glittering house. Jewels winked in every box, ladies craned their necks and men leaned over the ladies' heads to discover who was sitting with whom. Below them, the pit seethed with movement, laughter, and loud voices drifting upward. Above it all, the great chandelier shimmered in a rainbow of colorful sparks.

Mr. Marlowe turned his attention from the theater to Elizabeth. "Going back to our discussion of houses, perhaps I could drive you out to investigate the Richmond area."

"That would be very kind. As I said, Alice does not understand why I want a place for myself."

"I am not in any way implying criticism, Mrs. Drayton, but I wonder why you want to live alone?"

"Alice and Blaine ask the same question. But I have never tried it, and I want to have the opportunity."

"You want some independence."

"Yes, not for anything important, I suppose. But I

would like to take up my sketch pad and watercolors again. And perhaps see if I remember any of my lessons on the pianoforte."

"I assume while you lived with your husband's family, you could not do these things?"

She could hardly elucidate the discouraging atmosphere at Allward while sitting here amidst the magnificence of the theater. Who would believe the grimness she had endured? "I could not do much of anything. Even a walk on the moor was discouraged."

"So from that stultifying situation, you came to town and got tossed into Society's storm."

She smiled. "Yes, for Alice and her friends, there is one obligation after another, with a great deal of shopping included, not to mention the sightseeing. I have appreciated the efforts Alice and Blaine have made to make me feel part of their life—well, most of their efforts. But I am not sure I want to be so much a part of . . . of . . ."

"Of a life chosen by others. I am in very much the same situation. My sister claims she has my best interests at heart."

"Alice says exactly the same thing. She cannot imagine why I am not seeking a husband." Elizabeth nodded at a gentleman across the way who waved in her direction. Unless she was mistaken, it was Mr. Higgs, one of her most earnest pursuers.

"You have acquired many admirers. Certainly you must be flattered."

"On the contrary, I have no illusions about what most of them are after. There is a great deal of gossip about my supposed fortune, highly exaggerated I might add."

"You need to be especially careful, then."

"Yes, you must have a special understanding of the problem, Mr. Marlowe. I have noticed how some ladies treat you."

"It only shows they know nothing about me. Despite Faith's efforts, I have no intention of marrying again. Or becoming part of the leadership of Society. I am mostly content with my experiments and my specimens, except when I succumb to Faith's entreaties. As I explained, I have learned to be careful not to be caught alone with a lady and consequently expected to make an offer."

"Then, what must you have thought of me in the conservatory that first evening?"

"I could tell the moment I saw you that I need have no fears of entrapment from you."

"I should explain to you why I ran away so quickly that night. I was not afraid of being caught with you wholly on my own account. You see, because you were such a nice and charming man, I was sure you must be married. I thought that if those people coming into the conservatory saw us together, they would gossip and the matter would reach your wife's ears and hurt her."

"And that you would never do."

"I would not. It never occurred to me you might be in the same circumstance as I am, no longer married. Imagine my surprise when we were introduced a few nights later. I am sorry for your loss, of course," she added quickly. "How long . . ."

"My wife died two years ago."

"How very sad," she murmured.

"And your loss?"

"Last year in January. He was caught in a snowstorm and took a chill. I never expected . . ."

"How very sad for you."

She nodded. "When Reginald and I went to his home in Yorkshire to stay, I did not adjust well to living with his mother and his brother's widow. They have made their mourning into their entire lives."

"Not a healthy situation for anyone."

"No, particularly for my nephew, Richard, the young earl. I am most anxious that he comes to Eton to school soon."

"Yes, a house of perpetual mourning would not be a good place for a child."

"When I find a house, I hope he can visit me."

"I am sure he will. Have I told you how lovely you look tonight? That is a handsome gown."

Elizabeth had forgotten her low neckline and suddenly felt a twinge of discomfiture. "Ah . . . thank you." Her hands ached to give the dress an upward tug, but she dared not.

"You were saying you want a house now where you can be yourself."

A much safer subject, she thought. "Yes, Alice thinks I am wrong-headed. She believes I will be lonely."

"But instead, you will be able to have your life arranged just as you wish it to be."

"You understand, then?"

"I have found being alone and in charge of my own schedule quite freeing. As for the solitude, it can be quite comfortable. If one is in danger of feeling lonely, one can simply go visiting, in one's own good time."

"I look forward to a bit of solitude."

Blaine made a great deal of noise as he opened the door, calling back to Alice to hurry.

Elizabeth grinned behind her fan. As if she and Mr. Marlowe could have been interrupted doing anything untoward in this well-lit box in the sight of the entire assembly.

Alice and Lady Powell returned to their seats, both talking at once but throwing glances at both Elizabeth and Mr. Marlowe as if their somewhat private encounter would have left telltale signs on their faces.

At the conclusion of the evening's presentations, they joined the throng on the pavement outside. Sir James gestured to his carriage, among the tangle of equipages snarling the street. "Ride with me, if you please, Blaine. I wish to continue the conversation." Faith followed her husband into the Powells's carriage.

"I will see Alice and Mrs. Drayton home," Harry said.

Elizabeth and Alice got into the Gifford carriage, but before they could even begin to maneuver out of the traffic, Alice tapped on the ceiling of the coach to signal the driver, opened the door, and stepped out. "I just remembered what I had to say to Faith. Good night, Mr. Marlowe. It has been a lovely evening."

"But, Alice—" Elizabeth began to speak, but the carriage door slammed.

Harry opened a window and leaned out to see that Alice made it safely to the other carriage, then closed the window again against the midnight chill. He gave a little laugh. "So, once again, Mrs. Drayton, we are left alone."

Elizabeth pulled the rug over her knees. "Why, it is shocking indeed, is it not?"

She spoke as if in jest. But in truth, she was stunned at the situation. Unlike the brightly lit theater or the open doors of the drawing room at the Powell residence, the carriage was small and dark. The only warmth against the cool night air came from two wrapped bricks on the floor and from their bodies. She tried not to shiver but the more she attempted it, the more inevitable her eventual shaking became.

As she knew he would, Mr. Marlowe moved closer and placed his arm around her shoulders.

"I quite enjoy being alone with you, Mrs. Drayton."

"Are you saying you put my cousin up to her little trick?"

"Why, no. To be truthful, I hadn't the foresight."

She laughed aloud. "Did you enjoy the opera?"

"I most enjoyed our interlude alone in front of all those people. That was fun."

"Knowing anyone could be watching, yet being able to speak our minds without fear of being overheard."

"Perhaps we should play along with them, Mrs. Drayton. If we pretend to be considering a betrothal, we might have a great deal of relief from these awkward intrigues."

Elizabeth gasped. "Do you think anyone would be deceived?"

"That would depend on our ability to perform our roles as lovers."

Heat built in her veins. "I could never call myself an actress."

"But you must admit our time together has been quite agreeable. Think of all the unwelcome suitors you would avoid if they thought you were about to be married."

She smiled, fighting off a desire to giggle childishly. "I never would have thought of such a thing."

"Give it a little time, and see what you think."

When the carriage lurched forward, she was thrown against him and he tightened his arm, holding her close and drawing his cloak around her. "Is that better?"

She was sure he could hear her heartbeat thumping like a drum. "I am fine, thank you." She perceived a faint, exotic scent to him, as if some of the plants he tended gave him their perfume.

He was silent for a moment, and she wondered if he was reconsidering his outrageous suggestion.

"You know, Mrs. Drayton, the more I think on it,

the more I think such a pretend betrothal would be a very good idea. No more Sir Ennis for you. And I would be free of those mamas trying to trap me into a compromising spot."

Nestled here in his arms, she found her voice hard to summon. She managed just a murmur. "I believe you are serious, Mr. Marlowe."

He lifted her hand and held it near his lips. "I am serious." He touched his lips to her glove, his breath warm and stirring, then caressed her cheek with his thumb. "I would not find it difficult to treat you like my betrothed."

She could find no words to utter.

His voice was low, barely a whisper. "Think about it and when we meet tomorrow evening, we can reconsider the possibilities."

Seven

Elizabeth sat on her bed, her gown unlaced but still in place. She had sent Lolly away once the tapes were loosened. For the moment, Elizabeth wanted only to be alone.

Her head spun, from one thought to another image to a third, a fourth, and beyond with reckless speed. The drawing room. The theater box. The darkness of the carriage with his arm pressed against her side. Every nerve in her body seemed fevered, every sense sharpened.

What Harry suggested seemed impossible, yet excessively tempting. As he said, they enjoyed an amiable time together; they would ease the pressure from their good-hearted, if pushy, relatives, and they would be saved from the unwanted attentions of a variety of would-be romancers.

She sank back against the pillows and let her mind swirl.

Here she was, practically a new person, instead of the biddable girl that had entered an arranged marriage almost without a second thought, the docile wife that honored her husband's every request, the dutiful daughter-in-law. Now she was practically a rebel, forging a new life and finding new depths of courage and determination within herself.

At the tap on her door, she sat up stiffly, aware she had not stirred for a long time.

Without waiting for permission, Alice burst into Elizabeth's bedchamber, clad in her dressing gown, her long hair neatly braided. "Dearest Lizzie, tell me. Tell me everything that happened."

Elizabeth shook herself out of her stupor. "Not a word from me, you conniving rascal. Both you and Blaine deserve to be pilloried for such traitorous schemes, leaving me alone with Mr. Marlowe not once or even twice but three times. Whatever were you thinking?"

Alice widened her big blue eyes. "I cannot imagine what you mean. We had no such intentions."

"So, it was just a coincidence the four of you trotted out of Lady Powell's drawing room on some pretense. And you sped from our box at the opera, leaving us behind. And then you jumped out of the carriage. It would have served you right if you had fallen into the horse droppings."

Alice threw back her head and giggled. "I left the stair down when I entered the first time! I would not be so foolish as to—"

"So, you acknowledge it was all planned in advance!"

"I admit nothing. But what are you doing sitting on your bed without even calling your maid? Dreaming of a few kisses from Harry?"

"No, most assuredly not. Lolly loosened my ties before I sent her away."

"Here, let me help you." Alice unpinned the circlet of flowers from Elizabeth's blond hair. "The reason we did not let anyone into the box was that Mrs. Fitzmaurice-Smythe was about to enter with her frumpy daughter, and Sir Ennis was striding in our direction, as was Mr. Higgs. In fact, the traffic coming to our box was worse than outside after the performance, when everyone was trying to get to their carriages."

Elizabeth stood and let her gown slither to the floor in a puddle of graceful silken folds before she stepped out of it. She picked it up and ran her hands over the cool smoothness. She remembered his assured look, the gray glow of his eyes. . . . She turned to Alice. "But to leave us alone . . ."

"Admit it, you both enjoyed yourselves, did you not?"

"Mr. Marlowe is a most agreeable fellow."

"Lizzie, did you see the way he looked at you? His eyes were positively glued to your bodice."

Elizabeth pressed the handfuls of silk to her chest. "Oh, Alice, I told you it was too low."

"Not for a moment. Most of my gowns are much lower than that one."

Elizabeth turned toward the mirror and let the gown slowly slide to the floor again. The bodice really had not been particularly revealing, but even so, the thought of Harry Marlowe staring . . .

She picked up the dress and tossed it on the bed. Alice handed her a dressing gown, and Elizabeth slipped into it, then sat again, slowly plucking the pins from her hair.

Alice shook out the gown and hung it in the clothespress. "Faith says that Harry has been chased by some of London's most skillful flirts. She believes you are perfect for him."

"So, she conspires with you to compromise us?"

"Oh, nonsense. What is compromising about being in his sister's house with your own cousin or sitting in a theater box in front of a thousand people?"

"But what about riding in a dark carriage?"

"Lizzie, both of you have been married. Neither of you is a child. Even so, not a soul in London beyond our party knew you two were alone after midnight on the soft cushions in the darkness for a half hour. Whether or not you took advantage of a few moments of privacy is no concern to anyone but yourselves." Alice paused and peered intently at Elizabeth. "Of course, you must tell me."

Elizabeth could not help laughing. It was so like Alice to expect an account of every one of the thirty minutes. "Even if there were anything to tell, I would not say a word. But I assure you Mr. Marlowe was a perfect gentleman."

"Oh, that is odious! How utterly disappointing."

"I am sorry you have nothing to share with Blaine tonight, Alice. You two will have to make your own little amusements."

"Why, Elizabeth, whatever are you implying?"

Elizabeth gave an elaborate shrug.

Alice was not through yet. "Certainly he must have kissed you?"

The warm imprint of his mouth through the delicate kidskin of her glove still tingled, and she ran her fingers over the place his lips touched. She still felt the heat inside her, and knew it spread to her cheeks. She forced her voice to be steady and feigned boredom. "Alice, you are a thorough pest!"

"Is that a blush I see? So, he did kiss you."

"Of course he did. On my glove." She would not allow herself to touch the spot again.

"Oh, pooh. Faith will be exceedingly distressed."

Elizabeth pursed her lips and glowered at her cousin. "Not if you avoid telling her."

"But we promised—"

"Aha! You promised what?"

Alice looked away. "We thought . . ."

"What *were* you thinking? Certainly you knew you could not catch us in some rash indiscretion and force us to marry. What would be the point?"

"None whatsoever." Alice rose and blew Elizabeth a kiss. "You might not be surprised to know we shall keep trying."

Elizabeth made a face at her cousin, but Alice was through the door before she saw it.

So, Alice, Blaine, Sir James, and Lady Powell had more plans in store for her and Mr. Marlowe. Whatever would they think of the proposal he had made tonight?

Elizabeth turned down the lamp and climbed into bed, her head still awhirl with confused images.

Elizabeth followed the footman up the grand staircase of Lady Daveny's sumptuous townhouse.

Alice came along behind, rummaging in her reticule. "I had a handkerchief in here someplace, but I cannot find it."

Elizabeth stopped on the landing to tug out a hankie.

From above, she heard laughter.

A lady's voice was clearly audible. "She is very pretty."

Elizabeth handed the handkerchief to Alice and continued to listen to the conversation.

A brisk contralto chimed in. "Yes, and rich, they say. She has been attracting a great deal of attention among the gentlemen."

Now, a higher pitch. "Yes, that is so. They say Sir Ennis is quite smitten. And Mr. Higgs, though I doubt he really wants another wife."

Elizabeth glanced at Alice, who was as intent on listening as she was.

"Then is he in town just for the daughter?"

"Perhaps."

"Mrs. Drayton dresses well, if modestly."

"Not in the height of fashion."

"But not shabby."

"By no means."

Alice, a sour look on her face, grabbed Elizabeth's

hand and yanked her forward. "Thank you, James."
Alice practically shouted at the footman as they shot
into the drawing room.

But when she greeted the ladies, Elizabeth noted
with amusement, Alice was all sugar and cream.

"Good afternoon, Hortensia. Charlotte. Lady
Morris. Are all of you acquainted with my cousin,
Mrs. Drayton?"

Lady Daveny came forward and seized Elizabeth's hand. "It is lovely to see you again. How are
you? We were just talking about, ah, about Miss
Thorpe, a sweet thing, would you not agree?"

Elizabeth curtsied. "I am afraid I am not acquainted with the young lady." She sat down, her
heart thumping. How harrowing to overhear one-
self as the object of tittle-tattle. Was this dress not
quite the first stare? Of course it was not. She had
no ambition to be a fashion leader, and so she had
told Alice's dressmaker.

Two of the ladies quickly made their departure,
leaving Alice and Hortensia in earnest conversation, about what Elizabeth could not say.

It was not the fashion comment that stuck in her
mind. It was the mention of the money that she
most detested. There was one way to prevent herself from being the object of their chatter. If she
agreed to the sham betrothal with Mr. Marlowe, the
talk would continue for a day or two, then fade
away. A stale story was soon forgotten.

Mr. Marlowe bowed to Elizabeth. "I believe this
is our waltz, Mrs. Drayton." He wore a handsome
coat in a shade of blue so dark it appeared almost
black. His waistcoat was an understated shade of
ivory and a signet ring his only jewelry. His smile
was as warm as ever, but not a hint of his and

Elizabeth's conspiracy showed in his face. Not even a lifted eyebrow gave anything away to Alice's sharp eye.

Elizabeth stood and accompanied him to the floor where several couples were already dancing to the distinctive rhythm of the string orchestra. "I am rather a beginner at the waltz."

"You probably are more accomplished than I am," he replied. "But if we hide ourselves in the middle of this crush, we will not be revealed in our inelegance."

As she expected, his words were typically self-effacing, for he danced admirably and she could follow easily. He steered her through the crush past a dozen couples to the far side of the ballroom and outside onto a little terrace.

"Perhaps we can steal a few moments alone, Mrs. Drayton." They moved apart and walked to the balustrade. "I trust you have thought over our little scheme?"

She breathed deeply. "Yes, I have. I admit it has many advantages, a very tempting idea. But I wonder if it will be as easy as you say to convince people. My cousins will rejoice, but what will your friends say, those in the horticultural society?"

"They will wish me well, not that their opinion would matter anyway."

"So, you have no reservations?"

"None whatsoever."

She paused, nodding. She did have reservations but not the kind he probably thought of.

He stared out into the moonless night. A couple strolled on the dark lawn. "I hear in your voice a very large exception looming. You are about to say '*but*' . . ."

She laughed to fulfill his expectations. "You are correct. The problem I see is at the end. I . . . I wonder how we will end the charade. When, in a few months, we have not, ah, contracted a true betrothal, how will we explain things to our relations . . . to our friends? Will it not appear one of us has jilted the other? I fear I might be the one who would have to call off the betrothal, not an act I would relish. And it would please you even less, I suspect. To be branded the aggrieved party and be subject to the pity of all you know . . ."

"But if I had a good way to end it without hurting anyone and providing no more than a day's worth of gossip, would you then be agreeable?"

"Yes, I suppose. But, I cannot imagine . . ."

"You see, I am considering leaving on a voyage, a voyage to South America to collect botanical material, to be gone for several years. During that time, the separation will be too much. We can let the betrothal simply fade away. If you find another, in the meantime, there will be no problem explaining to people that we have had a mutual parting of the ways."

Elizabeth looked into his eyes crinkled in a smile. She shook her head a little and tried to sort out her thoughts, far too jumbled to comprehend. What would be the implications of such a plan and of its conclusion? She was unsure.

"Do not fret, my dear Elizabeth. Think of the pleasure we will give Faith and Alice."

"It sounds feasible, I guess."

"Then you say 'yes'?"

"As long as we an end it with neither of us called a jilt, I agree."

"Then I suggest we seal our bargain with a kiss. I believe that is the usual . . ."

He lowered his mouth to hers, sparking an instant explosion of light behind her closed eyelids. This was the danger point, the riskiest moment, when she could easily give herself to the trill of sensations that skittered through her veins.

When he released her, she watched his eyes, soft as they were in the dim light. What did he feel when he kissed her? To her, it seemed more than just a passing custom, a whimsical impulse.

She had no experience for this phase of the situation. From all that she had read and heard, it was the lady who set the boundaries of the caresses. But Elizabeth did not want him to stop kissing her.

She must. She pushed him away gently.

He continued to hold her in his arms. "I do not think we will be disappointed. Now we have to tell a very few people, and keep it very discreet."

She almost laughed out loud. "Discreet? Quiet? I thought the whole point is to keep our relations from foisting other prospects on us and to scare everyone off."

"Well, yes, but this way, in a matter of two days, or perhaps less, everyone will know—"

"Ah, I see. No formal announcement but an *on-dit* that will spread faster than honey in the hot sun."

"A lovely image that is . . . and precisely accurate, too."

"Mr. Marlowe—"

"Now that we are to be planning our betrothal, will you not call me Harry?"

"Harry—"

He lifted her hand and planted a kiss upon it, leaving a tingly spot she was tempted to press to her cheek. But she did not. "I'm willing to try, if you are."

Elizabeth wondered if her soaring pulse was a warning of potential danger. But the warm laughter she felt bubbling up inside carried away her fears.

Harry squeezed her hand. "Let us take one more day to think on it. I have a meeting tomorrow afternoon of the governors of the horticultural society. Tomorrow evening I will call for you before the musicale. We have one more opportunity to talk it over before we reveal our plans."

When they waltzed back into the ballroom, Sir Ennis was waiting for her at Alice's side.

"I believe the next set will be a country dance, Mrs. Drayton. A country dance. I hope you will favor me . . . favor me as a partner. A partner."

Beside her, Harry bowed to Sir Ennis and spoke softly in her ear. "There is your proof."

Elizabeth bit her tongue to keep from laughing as she took Sir Ennis's arm.

Eight

In Elizabeth's room, Alice balanced on the edge of a high stool, a method she used to minimize the wrinkles in her ice-blue silk gown. She watched Lolly pin the finishing curls into Elizabeth's blond locks. "Lizzie, my fingers simply itch to chop off some of that hair. You need it thinned and shortened around your face."

"You and I must agree to disagree about my coiffure, Alice. I see no need to cut it to meet some passing craze."

A footman appeared in the open doorway. "Mr. Marlowe is in the drawing room for Mrs. Drayton."

"Thank you, Archer." Alice's eyes danced. "Oh, I know he is besotted, Elizabeth. You must waste not a moment before you go down. Hurry, Lolly."

"Would I not appear overeager?" Elizabeth stared into the mirror, hoping her rapid pulse and the glow spreading through her did not show. Indeed, she *was* eager, eager to know if Harry had changed his mind. She still had her doubts, not the least of them the fear she might grow to care for him too much.

"At this stage of a romance, a touch of fervor seems called for, Lizzie. Blaine and I will be down shortly. Now, do not take the time to put on your gloves up here, silly. You can do that when we get our cloaks. Just grab your reticule and go!"

Elizabeth picked up her gloves and reticule, shaking her head at Alice. "You are incorrigible."

As she descended the staircase, she once more ran through all the arguments for and against the pretend betrothal. Her conclusion never varied. The advantages always trumped the disadvantages. Now, the question was whether Harry had come to the same conclusion. Or had he found some disadvantage they had overlooked before?

She paused in the doorway to read his expression. When he broke into a wide grin, her heartbeat switched from a rapid pace to a deep, steady thump.

"Good evening, Mrs. Drayton," he said and made a deep bow. He came forward as she curtsied and caught her hand, lifting it to his lips.

She almost dropped her gloves. His breath on the bare skin of her hand and the whisper-soft brush of his lips stirred her to the core.

She struggled to compose herself. This sense of excitement was quite unsuitable to the occasion. Completely out of keeping with a sham. "I trust your meeting was productive this afternoon?"

"It is always a privilege to spend time with Sir Joseph. He is knowledgeable on many levels, foremost among them botany, but on many other levels as well. He and his ladies—"

"Ladies? He has more than one?"

Harry chuckled. "As a matter of fact, he has two. His wife and his sister, Miss Sophia, have lived with him, in apparent harmony, for decades."

"I am greatly relieved. For a moment, I worried that he had picked up some very bad habits on his voyages."

Again Harry smiled and shook his head. "No, nothing so exotic as that. They appear to be a devoted trio. They will be moving to their summer home in Spring Grove next week. I hope I will have the opportunity to take you to visit there."

"I would like that."

"Then I will make the arrangements."

"Thank you."

He gestured to the sofa. "Perhaps we should make our final decision."

She took the place he indicated, and he sat beside her.

"Do you have any further thoughts on the matter, Mrs. Drayton?"

"No, though I admit my decision is greatly influenced by the fact I would no longer have to put up with some of the gentlemen who press their attentions so vigorously . . . Perhaps I am still overlooking other drawbacks."

"I have searched my mind for these drawbacks, but I, too, fail to find them."

Elizabeth could not stop the grin from starting.

He reached for her hand again. "Then, we have a bargain?"

"I am agreeable."

"Then, my dear, I believe it is appropriate to seal our contract with a kiss?"

Before she could answer, he leaned toward her and met her lips with his. His arms crept around her shoulders and she melted against his chest. Every nerve in her being sang out at the feelings that coursed through her. When at last he released her, she felt weak with delight.

The way he looked at her made her cheeks burn and her toes curl, but she did not move for several moments.

Finally, he broke the spell. "I brought you some flowers."

She looked around the room and saw only a few

familiar bouquets, all of which had arrived before she was even out of bed. "You did?"

He took a small velvet box from his pocket and opened it. Inside were earrings in the shape of five-pointed flowers with petals of cloisonné and centers of minute diamonds surrounding sapphires. On several of the petals, tiny pearls imitated drops of dew.

"Harry, they are beautiful. Quite exquisite. But you did not need—"

"Of course I did not need to buy them, but I had a lovely time shopping for them. I believe it was the first time in my life I enjoyed being at a jeweler's."

Elizabeth felt her throat thicken and tears threaten. She pushed the feelings aside. "They are the loveliest I have ever seen. May I wear them?"

"I want to see them in your ears," he said, leaning closer.

She handed him the simple pearls she unhooked from her ears.

"I hope it does not upset you to replace ear bobs your husband must have given you."

She felt a stab of surprise. It had not occurred to her. Not even a hint of feeling toward Reginald's long-ago gift. "Why, no . . . I am quite entranced with these lovely flowers. I suppose I do not dare ask you their name?"

"I believe they are fanciful creations, not specifically based on any particular bloom."

"I love them." She cradled them in her hand and held them close to a lamp, watching the light dance over them. "The problem with earrings is that once they are on, I cannot see them anymore."

"The more dazzling you are to those who have the privilege of gazing at you, my dear."

"Harry, I do appreciate this lovely gift, but if you persist in making such silly pronouncements . . ." She let the statement dangle, as he looked ready to speak again. She held up her forefinger and waggled it at him. "Do not dare to embroider further on your nonsense."

"I cannot promise not to flatter you a little from time to time."

"Only a little, then, just to keep up the pretense." She hooked the golden wires through her ears and admired the result in the mirror. She turned her head from side to side, watching the light sparkle from each flower.

"Yes, I found exactly the thing to best complement your beauty, my dear."

"Harry, I am warning you!" She heard Alice and Blaine creep down the stairs. "Shall we ride along with them, or do you have a carriage?"

"We can go with them, but first I want a proper thank-you."

He held out his arms, and without thinking, she moved into them and he clasped her hard against his chest, then tipped up her chin and pressed his lips to hers. His hand at her back held her close. She gave herself to the kiss and heard a little moan, knowing it was from herself.

When she pulled away, she had to swallow hard to push back the emotions that threatened to engulf her.

He whispered into her hair. "I will tell Faith in strict confidence tonight after we return home that we are considering a betrothal in a few months."

"I will tell Alice the same thing."

"And by tomorrow, it will be the talk of the ton."

Elizabeth laughed and preceded him into the hall.

In the bustle of entering the carriage, the usually sharp-eyed Alice did not notice Elizabeth's new jewelry. Just as well, Elizabeth mused as she arranged her cloak around her.

Not until the performance was concluded and

everyone filed in for refreshments did Alice give a little gasp. She leaned close and whispered in Elizabeth's ear. "Are those new ear bobs? I have never seen them before."

"I'll explain later." Elizabeth knew from the expression of dawning recognition on Alice's face that she had guessed where the little jewels had come from.

"From Mr. Marlowe?" Her voice almost squeaked with excitement.

Elizabeth let the movement of the crowd carry her away from Alice. Elizabeth gave a little wave and mouthed, "Later."

Mr. Marlowe caught up with her in the crush near a table of little cakes. He carried two glasses of champagne. "I consider this a just reward for enduring that greasy fellow at the end."

"He is supposed to be the big attraction."

"Folk songs from the Carpathian Mountains? I thought they would never end."

"Shush, Mr. Marlowe. Someone will overhear."

He lowered his voice a little more. "Who convinces Society hostesses to foist these characters on their friends? I suspect he is a complete fraud, probably hails from a Cornish village."

"I do not know what you are complaining about. I saw you and Blaine standing in the back when he began, but you were gone well before it was over."

Before they could finish their champagne, they were encircled by friends and drawn apart into separate conversations.

Harry's arm was gripped from behind and he heard the hiss of his sister's whisper in his ear.

"What is this about ear bobs?"

He turned to her with a grin. "Ear bobs?"

"Alice Gifford was so excited she could hardly talk. Did you present Mrs. Drayton with some jewelry, Harry?"

He nodded.

Eyes narrowed and mouth wide open, she could hardly speak herself. "Why did you not tell me? I did not know what Alice was talking about."

Harry looked around him. Faith's evident agitation had attracted some attention. "We cannot discuss it here. I will stop by Mount Street later, after I have seen Mrs. Drayton home with the Giffords."

"Harry, you are the most exasperating . . ."

He gave a little wave and kissed her cheek. "Have patience, sister, dear."

Clearly, patience had not taken root with Faith when he arrived in her drawing room more than an hour after they left the musicale.

"Where have you been, Harry? I have been absolutely unable to stand still. Poor James went off to bed. Said I made him jumpy."

Harry took a glass of brandy from the butler. "Thank you, Phipps. Now, what has you in such a state, Faith?"

"When Alice Gifford started talking about ear bobs, I had no idea what she meant."

"And you did not like her having the news first?"

She tossed her head. "Naturally, I hate being in the dark where my own brother is concerned."

He swirled the liquid in the glass and inhaled its aroma before taking a sip.

Faith stamped her foot. "If you do not explain yourself right this minute . . ."

"Yes? What makes you think there is anything important to explain?"

She flopped onto a chair. "Ooooh, Harry!"

"All right, I will tell you the whole story. I

happened to be strolling past a jewelry store the other day . . . and I wandered in . . ."

"Get to the point, if you please."

"As you say. I bought a pair of earrings for Mrs. Drayton."

"Harry! What does this mean?"

He shrugged one shoulder. "We are considering the possibility of becoming betrothed—"

"What?" She sprang to her feet. "That is wonderful. That is beyond marvelous. Does Alice know?"

"She did not earlier in the evening."

"Good!"

"I imagine when I left, Mrs. Drayton had a conversation with her cousin, a conversation very similar to this one. But you must not tell, Faith. As you know, Mrs. Drayton and I met just over a week ago. We think it will be wise to get to know one another. . . ."

She fairly quivered with delight. "Oh, naturally. But I am thrilled for you. I do not even mind sharing the matchmaker's role with Alice."

He tipped the last of the brandy past his lips. "I'll take my leave of you now, Faith, and walk home."

"But Harry, we have plans to make. And I want to hear more about what those ear bobs are like."

"Not now, my dear sister. I am ready to call it a night."

Her face fell. "Harry—"

"I'll be by tomorrow." But he doubted she would be at home. She had too many friends to whom she would need to divulge the news, in strictest confidence, of course.

All Mayfair would know before the coming day was out.

* * *

"Mrs. Drayton, ma'am, Mrs. Gifford asked me t' wake you. Lady Powell is 'ere. You're t' join 'em in the mornin' room."

"All right, Lolly." Elizabeth rolled over and pushed her face into the pillow. The clock chimed ten times, causing her to pull her nightcap over her ears to drown out the noise.

Whatever was Alice doing in the morning room two or three hours before she usually arose? And why was Lady Powell . . .

The recollection of last night slammed into her memory with the power of a swift arrow. The earrings. The dreadful concert. The champagne. Alice's exuberance.

Above all, that kiss. In nine years of marriage, Elizabeth had never been kissed like that before. Or more accurately, she had never felt from any of Reginald's attentions the kind of thrill she had from Harry's single kiss.

Later she would have to sort out her feelings about Harry's kiss. But now she had an ordeal ahead of her. Elizabeth knew that Alice and Lady Powell had some serious grilling in mind, and she better be on her toes. She had no intention of giving away the pretense. If she did, the whole charade would be exposed almost before it began.

"Good morning, my dear," Lady Powell got up and embraced her. "I cannot tell you how happy your betrothal has made me."

"I hope Mr. Marlowe explained that we are just considering a betrothal. We will wait a few months. To see how we rub along."

Lady Powell's laugh was like a tinkling bell. "Yes, that is exactly what Harry said."

Alice shook her head, a twinkle in her eye. "But think of the lovely earrings he gave you . . . What more evidence of his devotion do you need?"

"Exactly!" Lady Powell was just as emphatic as Alice.

"It seems accomplished in all but the formality."

Elizabeth looked from one to the other. "I believe there is a distinction to be observed, and we will take our time."

Both ladies lifted their eyebrows knowingly and exchanged grins.

Exactly as Elizabeth wished them to. She gave a tiny sigh of relief that she had made it through the first step.

"You have not known each other very long, but I could tell from the first moment you met, great things were ahead. I have prayed for Harry to find happiness and I think he has." Lady Powell settled back in her chair.

"Thank you."

"Knowing men, I doubt that he has told you much about his marriage. Caroline was not the kind of woman he needed, I am afraid. I should not speak ill of the dead, but I never wanted him to wed her in the first place. She was much too young and frail. Before a year passed, she became an invalid and so she stayed for the rest of her life."

Pity flooded into Elizabeth as Lady Powell spoke. "It must have been excessively difficult for both of them."

"Being a perfect gentleman, he never spoke a word against her. Never the slightest complaint. Most of us were convinced there was nothing seriously wrong with her. It suited her to concoct spasms and spells. Even the physicians agreed. So, when she finally became truly ill, she was beyond help by the time the doctors believed her."

"How sad."

"Well, yes, it was sad. He has been a widower now for several years, and I have been trying to get him out of his gardens and hothouses. He needs to be out and around."

Just how "around" would he be when he sailed off to Brazil? Elizabeth wondered how his sister would react when he made that announcement someday.

Alice was uncharacteristically quiet, taking in every detail.

Elizabeth hoped Lady Powell would continue. "He has not spoken much of his childhood."

"We grew up in Suffolk, a large family. We've been there for centuries, raising sheep for the most part. I have three sisters and five brothers. Harry is the youngest, but I should explain we have all been well provided for. My eldest brother, the twelfth baron, has thousands of acres. I cannot remember how many."

Alice poured Lady Powell another cup of tea. "How fascinating!"

Lady Powell accepted the cup. "What else can I tell you?

He is devoted to science. He not only makes my daffodils bloom in December and my roses bloom in January but also writes papers to present at the Royal Horticultural Society. Once he thought of himself as becoming a great botanist, but because of his wife's afflictions, he long ago reconciled himself to modest contributions to the growing body of knowledge in his field. He is a man of admirable balance."

"Lady Powell, I am glad you and your brother are so close."

"Now that we are about to be sisters, I hope you will call me Faith. And, if you agree, I will call you Elizabeth."

"I would like that very much, Faith."

"I am delighted you two have found one another. You are the kind of lady he needs. He does not gamble, nor does he yearn to own racehorses. I know of no one who dislikes him. He is held in high esteem among his friends."

Lady Powell beamed at Alice. "I think we can congratulate ourselves, Mrs. Gifford, Alice, I should say. We have been quite decisively clever."

"Indeed, my dear Faith, we have proved ourselves to be superior in the matchmaking field."

Elizabeth decided it was time to drop in a little reservation, just to make them even more positive of their success. "Please remember this is very tentative. Harry, ah . . . Mr. Marlowe and I are only thinking about a future betrothal. This is certainly not a sure thing."

As she had suspected, their knowing smiles showed that neither Alice nor Faith believed a word she spoke. *Excellent!*

"Now you must tell me about yourself, Elizabeth," Faith said. "I want to get to know you much better."

"I have led a very quiet life, especially since Reginald died. There is little to tell. Nothing interesting at all."

Alice broke in. "Your humility is admirable, dear cousin Elizabeth, but the parade of gentlemen you have attracted indicates a different conclusion."

Elizabeth cast her eyes downward. Perhaps she was not such a bad actress after all.

Faith shifted in her chair. "While I know it is highly improper to mention monetary matters, I hope Harry has told you he has a generous income." She looked embarrassed, giving a little cough before she went on. "I only say that because I have heard that you, Elizabeth, are quite wealthy. Harry does not need to marry a fortune, for he is plump in the pocket himself. I say this with the utmost discretion, but knowing Harry, I would not be surprised if he never mentioned the size of his purse."

Alice shook her head. "Yes, somehow Elizabeth's wealth got into general knowledge, and I am sure that Elizabeth would not deny it. I believe Mr. Marlowe's affluence is not as widely discussed."

Faith smiled. "But no less real. Now enough of that dreaded topic. I shall take my leave of you ladies. I have several calls scheduled, but I wanted to be the first to wish you well, Elizabeth."

Faith embraced her, and Elizabeth dared to make one last reminder, though she guessed it would be appropriately futile. "And, of course, you both will keep our secret?"

Both ladies nodded vigorously.

"You can count on us," Faith said as she hurried out, eager, Elizabeth thought, to spread the news.

Alice took a last swallow of her tea. "If you wish to rest today, Elizabeth, I shall quite understand. I have a few stops to make this morning, and I am sure they would be nothing but fatiguing to you."

Elizabeth stifled her laughter. "You go right ahead, Alice. I would welcome a restful day." *And I know my presence would inhibit your ability to whisper the very confidential information you have to impart!*

Harry had been quite correct in his scheme. The news would travel ever so much faster if given in strict secrecy!

Elizabeth curled up in a chair in her room and gazed out the window at the tiny garden behind the house.

She prayed she had done the right thing now that the die was cast. Harry had suggested the scheme and seemed pleased she had agreed. He was insulated from the ladies' pressures. He was going off on a long voyage in a few months. He had no worries.

She, too, was insulated from the imprecations of

the gentlemen. But there was a danger at hand. Her heart could be at risk. Her head told her she had no reason to be concerned. Yet, she knew how she reacted to him. She felt alert in a special way when he was around. Her feelings, her emotions, her body became specially attuned to his. Last night, they all betrayed her.

If she was to survive the next few months with her heart intact, she needed to talk herself into a calmer reaction to him. Her eagerness to have her independence was unchanged, so she could not let her friendship with Harry go any further. Kisses were out of bounds. She could not allow herself to fall in love.

For men, it was different, or so she had heard from other females and had read in novels. Men could make love without engaging their hearts. For a woman like her, the stakes were different. If she allowed her feelings to get out of bounds, if she followed her heart without heeding her good sense, this sham betrothal could be the worst thing she had ever done.

Would Harry understand if she told him this? No, it was best not to let him know how worried she was, better to keep her fears to herself. Now she had another secret to protect, this one even more crucial.

Nine

Elizabeth wished she had a carriage dress in a slightly lighter shade of green than the one she wore. She turned before the cheval glass in her bedchamber. The simple cut suited her, but the color . . . She mentally laughed at herself. She was beginning to think like Alice, as if fashion actually meant something real rather than being a passing fancy of wealthy women with too little to think about.

She had quite enough in her brainbox without worrying about clothing. In the three days since she and Harry had confided their intention to become betrothed at some unspecified future date, she had received the intimate congratulations and best wishes of practically everyone she had met in London, not to mention quite a few callers she did not remotely remember encountering before. Alice, while never admitting to informing a soul of the secret, presided over the guests with glee, proud of her matchmaking.

Lady Addie, Mrs. Berwald, and Mrs. Welk had actually called twice, not wanting to miss any of the details of the unfolding romance.

Now the moment she had been waiting for was almost here. Mr. Marlowe would take her to see a few houses in the Richmond area, ten or twelve miles west of London.

Alice tapped at the door and called to her. "Elizabeth, are you going house hunting again?"

"Come in, Alice. Yes, I am going to look at some more houses."

"Why, when you will soon be married?"

Elizabeth hesitated, wondering how to answer, but fortunately, Alice chattered on.

"Do you wish to have me accompany you, just for the sake of appearances, that is? Of course, a chaperone is not really necessary, in view of the fact you are both widowed and almost betrothed. But perhaps I should go along."

Elizabeth bit back an instant refusal. "You are most welcome, but I will warn you we are going as far as Richmond."

"Why?"

"Because Mr. Marlowe is familiar with the area. He is involved with the botanical experiments at the gardens at Kew."

"Oh, I see. So, you are looking for a house for the two of you. Of course! Why did I not figure that out immediately? Sometimes I am as much a widgeon as Blaine says I am! How could I ever have thought you might want me along?"

Elizabeth hardly knew what to say.

Alice kissed her cheek. "I hope you and Mr. Marlowe find a perfect residence, even if it is so far away." With that, Alice bustled off.

Elizabeth stared at herself in the mirror. Since her agreement with Harry, there had been myriad unanticipated issues raised, questions about the future she had no idea how to answer. It was to be expected, she realized, that people would think every move either of them made would be considered as part of their eventual alliance.

She would have to work hard not to fall into the trap of thinking that way herself.

* * *

Harry strode to the mews, trusting that his groom and pair would be ready for their trip to look at houses in Richmond. He was due at the Giffords's in a half hour to call for Elizabeth. Though it was only a few streets distant, he wanted to be certain his curricle and the bays were in prime condition.

Al, his groom, buckled the last of the harnesses into place as Harry rounded the corner.

"They are looking good, are they not, Al?"

"Excellent, sir."

"I believe a few months on grass were good for them." Harry had sent the team to his brother's estate in Suffolk six months ago. He had rarely needed them, depending instead on his saddle horse. But now, if he was to drive Elizabeth around, he could not count on borrowing one of his sister's teams day after day.

Harry ran his hand along the shiny neck of the gelding he called Buck. "Are they rested after the journey?"

"Seems so to me," Al answered, giving a final shine to the brass trim on one of the bridles.

Buck turned his head, bits jangling, and looked for a treat, nudging at Harry.

"You, fella', have not changed your greedy habits." He took a piece of carrot from his pocket and held it for the soft lips of the gelding to grasp.

"And how about you, Al? Are you rested up? From the looks of the curricle, you have been up all night with a polishing rag."

"Not me, sir. But the stable boy scrubbed every one of them spokes. Even touched up the paint."

"Remind me, when we return, to thank him and pay him a bit extra."

"Yessir, I'll do that. He's a fine lad."

Harry gave a carrot to Tuck, the other tall bay, then helped Al back up the team to the curricle and fasten the traces.

In moments, with Al up behind, Harry headed the team toward Brook Street. He was truly looking forward to spending the day with Elizabeth. Since their agreement had become known—widely known, he thought to himself with a chuckle—they had spent little time alone, hardly enough for half a conversation. Wherever they went, well-wishers crowded round them, full of congratulations and full of questions. Both he and Elizabeth had become adept at the coy smile, the tiny shrug, the long pause. The more they dissembled, the more convinced their companions became that it was a match made in heaven.

Which, Harry thought as he negotiated a corner, was not far from the truth. He grew fonder of Elizabeth every day. More than once it had occurred to him they might make a true betrothal, but he held back. She wanted her independence, and he had to respect that.

He could hardly imagine how a young girl with no worldly experience would have reacted to an arranged marriage. Or how she had lived at Allward. From the little she had said about it, that grim house must have been a true prison to her. Little wonder that she craved freedom from the restrictions of another's dictates.

No, if he truly cared for her, he would follow her wishes and hope that after a few months, she might decide that independence might be continued with—or even enhanced by—a closer relationship with him.

He had begun to question his future plans. Gradually, he had come to regard his participation in the voyage as uncertain. His enthusiasm had faltered fur-

ther when the group had talked about extending the
expedition to Botany Bay and beyond, adding a probable third year. He would not yet disclose his doubts
to Elizabeth about leaving. He almost felt it would vi-
olate their agreement if he did. And the last thing
she needed to be concerned about was how the betrothal would end if he stayed right here in England.

For the time being, he could only depend upon
his patience, an essential quality for a botanist and
an essential quality for a lover as well.

When Harry arrived at Brook Street, Alice Gifford did not come down to greet him. Elizabeth
told him why, and they shared a good laugh as he
helped her into his curricle.

Before he picked up the reins, she took out some
papers from her bag. "These are the latest listings
sent by Mr. Lytton, all in or near Richmond, he
said. Do you know the locations?"

Harry glanced over the pages. "I cannot guaran-
tee I know them precisely, but I believe I can find
all three of these houses without too many wrong
turns."

"I so hope one of them will be suitable."

He clucked to his team, and his groom swung up
at the back. "If none of these will serve, we will keep
looking." He was quite willing to spend the next
four months driving her around.

Elizabeth folded her papers. "But you have other
things to attend to. I cannot take up all your time."

"Elizabeth, if I tell you it is my privilege, you will
accuse me of flummery again. So, I will merely say
that I am pleased to help."

"Thank you." She settled back, stuffed the papers
in her bag, and said no more.

Out of Mayfair, the traffic thinned and the carriage rolled along smoothly. Harry turned to her
with a grin. "Have you been busy with callers?"

"Yes, Lady Addie and Mrs. Welk have been by to offer their best wishes and to attempt to trap me into giving them all the details of the proposal."

"What did you tell them?" This was the first time he could remember that he wished he had been a party to a lady's afternoon call.

"There are times when my tendency to blush is useful."

"So, you lowered your eyes and smiled, with your cheeks glowing. Yes, that is a most attractive and pretty attribute."

"Now you are teasing me."

"I apologize, but I do enjoy seeing that pretty glow."

"Mr. Marlowe—"

"Harry."

"Harry, you do not need to flirt with me. After all, if people consider us betrothed . . ."

"Elizabeth, one of the advantages of being betrothed is spending time together, which we have agreed we enjoy, is that not so?"

"Yes, but this is a pretense. . . ."

"Which does not mean we have to make each other miserable."

Elizabeth could not help laughing. "This house-hunting venture has brought up a little problem I had not anticipated. Alice assumes the house I seek will be for the two of us."

"Of course she would."

"But, if I find something, how can we . . ."

"You can move in and live there, arrange it any way you want to. I will, of course, retain my rooms in Mayfair for the months ahead. And visit you frequently."

"You make it sound very simple."

"It is simple, my dear. In a few months, our consortium will announce the voyage to South America, and I will decide to go. No one will be surprised if our betrothal is never formalized, and by the time the ship returns several years later, it will be quite forgotten." He would not tell her of his growing reluctance to accompany the voyage. He did not want to upset their arrangement, not while he could be with her so often.

The day was bright, under thin clouds, with comfortable temperatures. As they traveled along the Richmond Road, they made good time. "Would you like to see a bit of the village before we look for the houses?" Harry asked.

"I would. I have never had the opportunity to see it, though I have been nearby."

"Centuries ago, there was a friary adjacent to the palace, but nothing remains of that. And Richmond Palace, the great edifice, was mostly demolished in the time of Cromwell. Queen Elizabeth died there in 1603."

When they reached the village, Harry walked the horses around the green.

Elizabeth was amazed. "These houses are huge."

Harry reined the team to a halt before a tall, stately red-brick structure. "Most of them around the green were built in the early eighteenth century by wealthy courtiers. Even though Richmond Palace was long gone, kings spent a great deal of time in residence at the royal hunting lodge."

They started up again and came to a short pavement beyond another magnificent residence. Harry pointed his whip. "The old Outer Gateway still stands."

"All alone, it hardly looks like the entrance to a fabled palace."

Harry turned the team and drove to a narrow lane beyond the gate. "This is another part of the old palace, the old wardrobe, with the typical

Tudor-era diagonal design of darker bricks against the red."

"You know a great deal about Richmond."

He laughed. "Not really. I have always found it a delightful village, but I admit to looking through a guidebook to find the details last night. I have a copy of the book for you, if you want it." He was very glad he had made the effort to read it.

"Oh, yes, very much. How very sweet of you to be my guide."

He pulled up alongside the river not far from the bridge. "Now, let's see if we can find the houses."

They consulted the map and Elizabeth's lists, finding the first two houses with no trouble. Both were attractive, but neither appealed to her.

The third house sat outside the town, upstream to the north. As they approached the site, they drove along a road halfway up the hill in view of the river. Coming through a grove of trees, they turned on a narrow drive marked Cloud Spring.

The moment the house came into sight, Elizabeth's breath quickened. It resembled her dream house, the house she had yearned for for months. A full six bays wide, it had a steep roof, almost in the style of Sir Christopher Wren. The closer they came, the brighter the sun grew until the clouds drifted off and the house fairly glowed in its brilliant rays. She had the distinct feeling she was coming home.

Behind the house, the wooded hill continued its rise. A cluster of outbuildings stood off to one side: a stable, a small carriage house, and beyond them, an orchard.

Elizabeth could not wait to see the inside. "Harry,

I like it very much." There was something about it, a feeling that she knew it already.

"Yes, it looks very promising." He drove up to the side door. "Whoa. We'll get out here, Al, and you can walk them for a few moments."

A man in work clothes appeared from the stables and waved. "Bring 'em this way. Gotta trough over here."

Elizabeth hopped to the ground and went up two steps to peer through the glass beside the door. Her pulse raced, and as a woman approached from inside, Elizabeth felt the excitement bubble up.

"Yes?"

"I am Mrs. Drayton, and this is Mr. Marlowe. We are here to see the house."

"Yes'm. Come in and look around."

Within five minutes, Elizabeth's best hopes were confirmed. The elderly lady said little, but the house spoke for itself.

It was far from grand, but it had well-proportioned spaces full of light. On the ground floor, there were a large drawing room, a library, and a morning room next to a small breakfast room, all with tall windows and an airy feel.

Outside the drawing room, she saw the remnants of an old parterre, including many spent tulips that must have been glorious a week or two before.

Harry motioned to the long windows. "They have done some refitting, for those look very much like the latest in French doors, as I have heard them called. They open onto the terrace."

"How lovely." Elizabeth turned the handle and pushed, and the window became a door, leading, as he had surmised, onto the flagstones outside.

She hardly knew where to turn next, to explore the garden or go upstairs. Her desire to see the bedchambers won out, and she headed up the staircase, a graceful example of the wood turner's art. As she had envisioned, there were four large rooms opening off a central hall that held a cabinet for linens and a door to the attics and servants' quarters.

Elizabeth felt a sense of peace steal over her; now for the first time in her life, she could have a home like this, make it her very own. Though it very much needed a loving mistress to give it fresh paint and perhaps some new wallpaper designs, it was essentially ready for her to move in.

As they toured the outbuildings, Elizabeth could see many possibilities and only a few drawbacks. An old cottage at the rear of the property was in disrepair, and the stable roof needed some new tiles.

Harry tucked her arm through his as they walked through the gardens. "Things out here need a bit of work, but I see good bones. With a couple of men, I could have things trimmed up and replanted in less than a week."

"But you would not have to . . ."

"It makes my fingers itch to see it this way. I would enjoy the project, and the time of year is just right."

"Then you agree with me? I could not imagine a house that I would like better."

"Yes, I can see from the look on your face that the deal will be closed before the week is out, Elizabeth."

Standing beside Harry, in the garden of Cloud Spring, Elizabeth felt her heart might burst with joy.

When she returned to Alice's house in Brook Street, Elizabeth could hardly wait to tell her cousin about the house. But instead of immediately regaling Alice and Blaine with her discovery, she sat down to read a letter waiting for her from Mr. Macneil at Allward.

She opened it quickly, hoping it brought good news.

Indeed, it was the best she could have hoped for. All the arrangements were in place for Richard to enter the summer term at Eton. The two of them would arrive in London in less than a month.

Only an hour after he had brought her back to Alice's, Harry returned to escort Elizabeth to a musicale.

She was doubly happy as she shared her news. "I am so thrilled. Richard needs to be with boys of his own age. He has lived with his mother and grandmother far too long and under conditions I consider too strict for any child."

"You mean he has no real friends among the boys of the neighborhood?"

"None. The dowager never agreed to it. I used to read him stories, and we made up some fanciful tales ourselves. I tried to make him laugh from time to time, but in that house, laughter was never tolerated."

"What of his mother? Certainly, she would not want him to be lonely and friendless."

"Hester is impossible for me to understand. She married the earl and bore him a son, but once her husband died, she became as absorbed in her grief as the dowager. The dowager cares deeply about Richard fulfilling his role as the earl but never thinks of him as just a boy. Hester never disagreed with her methods."

Harry assisted Elizabeth with her cape, they called good-bye to Alice, who was coming later, and went to his carriage, this time his sister's landau.

When the door was shut, he tapped on the ceiling and the coach moved off. "Living at Allward must have been difficult for you to endure."

"I could do so very little. Though I tried to make

Richard's life a little cheerier, I am not sure I
succeeded. But at last he will get out of that dreary
household and begin to learn about life outside."

"Eton may not be easy for him." Harry did not wish
to alarm her but thought a gentle warning was in
order.

"Oh, he is very bright."

"That is not exactly what I mean."

"Mr. Macneil will have prepared Richard well. He
was a king's scholar himself, one of the boys who attended because he was specially chosen for his
talents and abilities, not for his family status."

"I did not go to Eton, but I know a number of
men who did. They were all proud of surviving the
program."

"Yes, I understand the academics are rigorous."

Harry decided to go no further. Much of what he
had heard about the older boys teasing the younger
boys—and worse—might have been exaggerated.
And after all, Richard was an earl, not just any
common fellow.

"I look forward to meeting the boy."

"I hope you will take him to Kew to see your specimens. He was engaged last year on a project of
cataloging all the trees at Allward. I think you will
like Mr. Macneil, too, a fine young man with a deep
interest in botany."

"I shall take them both through the gardens any
time. Now, tell me about what Alice said when you
told her about Cloud Spring."

Elizabeth raised her eyebrows questioningly.
"What is your guess?"

"She thinks it sounds . . . ah, very distant?"

"Precisely. She simply rolled her eyes in wonder-
ment. It is the same old discussion. 'Why would anyone
want to live any place in the world but Mayfair?'"

Ten

"If Alice saw me, she would simply swoon." Elizabeth spoke out loud to herself as she tied a square of cotton around her head. An oversized apron protected her gown, and she wore an old pair of cast-off slippers she begged from Lolly. Her move was actually getting underway, and even the formidable tasks ahead could not dampen her joy.

In the kitchen below, Peg, her newly hired house-maid, was engaged in scrubbing the stove and the big wooden table. Two men-of-all-work had emp-tied the stable of debris and would shortly go off to buy a load of straw and hay.

After bringing her to Cloud Spring this morning, Mr. Marlowe had taken it upon himself to search for an easygoing carriage horse and a light gig she could drive herself. Later she could choose a quiet mount for outings in Richmond Park.

Elizabeth intended to dust the bedrooms herself, a perfect opportunity to judge each of the four chambers, their views, and their fittings to get a feeling for which she might choose for her own use. She enjoyed the exercise, feeling that at last she could begin to put her mark on the house she hoped would fulfill her dreams.

The first room, with a southeast exposure, seemed a likely sitting room. The paneling was handsome,

painted a now-dingy white with well-placed brass
sconces on each side of the marble fireplace sur-
round. She could almost see her collection of china
figurines on the mantel, that is, if those relics of her
childhood had survived their years of storage with
the furniture she and Reginald had put away for the
day when they could return to London. She had a
neat folder of receipts for the yearly charges.

The delivery would come tomorrow, and she
would begin to fill the rooms—if indeed the furnishings were intact, not full of dry rot or insect
damage after six years.

It had taken ten days of haggling between Mr. Lytton and the legal representatives of the owner,
untangling the deeds that removed the property
from the royal manor and other complications that
had tried Elizabeth's patience. But at last it became
official, and she had signed her name at least eleven
times to various documents that made Cloud Spring
hers.

Feather duster flying, she finished two walls and
turned to the third, noting the weak sunshine that
spread across the wide boards of the floor. They
needed a good scrub and a coat or two of wax. She
added that to her mental list for the men to accomplish this afternoon.

When she moved on to the other three bedchambers, she decided the paneled room could be
her personal studio where she would paint or read
in solitude, a private room for dreaming. A room
for her alone.

She could also see Mr. Marlowe here, perhaps
working with her at a table, learning to sketch
botanical specimens. He had said he was in need of
considerable practice, and this room might be a
place they could learn together.

She slapped her hand on the windowsill. What was

she thinking of to imagine Harry Marlowe sitting here with her? Before long, he would be half a world away. She was much too dependent on his good nature. But soon she would have to learn to do without his help. And his company.

She opened the window and shook the dust out of the feathers. She would hire a good staff and manage things herself, once she moved in. Yearning for Harry was something she could not afford.

The bedchamber she chose for herself was equal in size to the others and had a nice bow window right above the French doors in the drawing room, obviously a recent addition to the hundred-year-old structure. In that alcove, she could place a little table for writing letters or filling the pages of her journal.

The wallpaper was a quaint design, obviously new since the bow window was added and not in need of replacement.

The other two bedchambers needed freshening, and she added ordering samples to her mental list. One she would make Richard's room.

By the time Elizabeth came downstairs, Peg had two friends dusting and sweeping the dining room.

"Mrs. Drayton, these are the two I told you 'bout. Daisy and Molly." The two girls curtsied.

"Thank you for coming. As you can see, the house is in need of all the scrubbing we can give it."

She went to the small library at the rear of the house and added to her list of chores written on a tablet that sat on the empty bookshelves. What a delight it would be to purchase some volumes to fill them, a good history of England, for one thing. And a set of Shakespeare's plays. An atlas so that she could have Mr. Marlowe show her where he had traveled on his voyage to South America and where he might go on his upcoming trip.

Elizabeth had no experience of sea travel, not even across the Channel to France, but she envisioned the hardships as described by others and felt she was better off staying home. Except that she would like to see Paris. And Rome. And Venice, even Constantinople.

But first she would make herself a real home here, in this house for which she already felt affection. Her life would change when she lived here. Distance, as well as her sham betrothal to Harry, would free her from the daily round of calls received and calls to make as well as free her from the nightly procession from rout to rout. Harry was as delighted as she was to send his regrets to eager hostesses.

"Mrs. Drayton!" One of the maids called to her from the entrance hall. "You have a visitor."

Elizabeth lifted the dust protection from her hair and began to untie her apron as she went to the front door. She was surprised to see a young lady standing there, a straw bonnet in her hand.

"I beg your pardon for interrupting you, Mrs. Drayton, but I could not wait to come over and welcome you to the parish. I am Sarah Iveson, the vicar's daughter, and everyone calls me Sally."

"Please come in, Sally. You are my first visitor."

The young lady turned and spoke to someone beside her. When Elizabeth looked out, she saw it was a large dog, which lay down in the shade and looked comfortable staying put.

Elizabeth opened the door, and Sally entered the house. "I was so hoping I would be first. I am happy someone will be living here at Cloud Spring again. It has been empty for more than a year, and I have missed coming here. You see, the daughter of the house was almost my age. This is a very happy house, you know. The previous owners came into a handsome inheritance and moved to an estate in Kent, where I visited last March."

Sally paused for a breath and plunged on. "Father said he would pay you a call next week when you are settled, but I could not wait. Is it true you will live here alone?"

"Well, yes—"

"I think that is most clever of you. If I am ever a widow, I will most certainly not live with—oh, pardon me. I should not discuss such a subject. I do tend to chatter, my father says, but I should not be so forward. Can I tell you anything about the house? I know every nook and cranny of all the buildings and the grounds as well."

"Then perhaps you can explain to me why it is called Cloud Spring."

"Have you seen the spring? It is quite small but was running clear the last time I was up there."

"So, there really is a spring!" Elizabeth was truly pleased.

"Oh, yes. But about the Cloud part, the owners long ago were the Lowds. Over the years, instead of Lowd Spring, which sounds so raucous and is not at all true, the name gradually changed to Cloud Spring, which, I am sure you will agree, is a most melodious and beautiful name."

Elizabeth laughed. She was going to enjoy having Sally as a caller. Now there was no doubt in her mind that she would never be lonely at her new residence, not with Sally nearby.

"It is simple to find. There is a little path behind the well house. Would you like to see it now?"

"Why, yes, I would." Elizabeth hung her apron on the doorknob and followed Sally across the terrace and through the garden. The dog, a mixed breed of no particular beauty, trotted after them.

"I call him Corky. He has an uncanny way of

knowing people. If he growls at someone, that person must be a rogue. He never barks or chases rabbits unless we are in the park. Then he is like a wild puppy again."

Sally stopped and examined a tangled rosebush with more dead branches than buds. "This was once a very pretty garden, but it has sadly gone wild. I imagine you will be busy here this summer."

"No doubt." To Elizabeth, it looked to need at least a half dozen gardeners, but perhaps it was only the seasonal exuberance of the plants as they responded to the warming weather. Now that it was hers, the task of shaping it into a pleasant bower seemed far more daunting.

Beyond the garden, a path curved up the hill and toward a clump of brush. As they walked through more shrubbery, they passed a small well house of the same brick as the main house but covered with thick ivy.

Nearly obscured by low-hanging branches, Elizabeth saw the opening of a cavern. Sally pushed the boughs aside and led the way into a grotto with damp and mossy walls. A small spring bubbled in a stone basin then spilled over and ran off between the cracks of the floor.

"The water is warm," Sally said, dipping her hand into it. "But not as warm as the baths in town."

Elizabeth tried it and, indeed, it was warm to the touch. "I was not aware that there were hot springs in Richmond."

"Oh, yes, nothing like Bath, but they attract some invalids to town. Once there was a fancy resort here, but it was closed a long time ago. Father says they gambled there. I have heard there are other springs still flowing, but yours is the only one I know."

Corky licked at a little pool, then stopped and shook himself, as if to censure the water itself.

Elizabeth watched him with amusement. "It looks like Corky does not savor the water. Have you tried drinking it?"

"Oh, no. It tastes terrible, or so they say. Some of the people around here claim it will cure anything, but I am never sick, so I have not tried it."

As they walked back to the house, Sally continued to tell Elizabeth about her family, her brother at Oxford, and a younger sister, also away at school. "I am almost sixteen and so I am allowed to stay with Father and keep house for him."

"I hope you will come back to visit me again soon." Elizabeth spoke with real conviction. "I want to learn all about the parish and the town. And perhaps you can help me find a bookshop and a stationer."

"Oh, I should love that, Mrs. Drayton."

Sally called to the wandering Corky, but before she could start down the lane, Mr. Marlowe's pair of tall bays were nearing the house.

Al hopped down to take the horses' heads as they came to a stop.

Harry stepped out of the curricle. "I found you a hardy chestnut with gentle manners and a nice gig."

"Thank you, Harry. Miss Iveson, this is Mr. Marlowe. He and I are . . . are considering becoming betrothed."

Sally curtsied. "I am pleased to know you, Mr. Marlowe. I have been bothering Mrs. Drayton for the past hour."

Elizabeth and Sally exchanged a quick glance as Corky trotted toward Harry, panting, then paused and looked him over.

"Hey, boy," Harry said, reaching toward the dog. Corky went to him, tail wagging vigorously.

Sally giggled. "You have passed muster, Mr. Marlowe."

Elizabeth grinned too. "Corky is a renowned and perceptive judge of character."

"Then I shall borrow him to take along on my next expedition to buy a horse. I could have used some help measuring the truth of the owners' descriptions of their animals."

When Sally had gone and Harry had accompanied Al and the horses to the stable, Elizabeth sat down on the steps. She was glad she had worn an old gown, for the twigs had snagged the fabric in several places. When she and Harry returned to London, Alice would be aghast.

Harry took a seat beside her. "One more theatrical night to sit through, and we can have some free evenings."

"Yes, as we expected, people have lost interest in us. I must say, it has been simpler than I anticipated."

"You mean acting as though we are betrothed?"

Elizabeth brushed at a thread on her skirt. "Yes, I have found that the more I protest and remind people the agreement is only tentative, the more they roll their eyes and pat my hand."

He got to his feet. "If I even hint we might not go through with the proposal, the men slap me on the back and laugh out loud."

Elizabeth winced a little as she laughed. She thought she knew her own mind when she came to London. Now, in a few days, whether she really wanted it or not, she would have her long-desired independence.

In Brook Street that evening, as they dined before going to the theater, Elizabeth told Alice about her day.

Alice was shocked. "One maid and two girls from the village? You will also need a personal maid, and Mr. Marlowe will need a valet."

"Peg says she has a younger sister who is good with hair and loves to sew and care for gowns. She can come in a few days a week. As for Mr. Marlowe, he shares a valet with a neighbor now, but I am sure he is quite capable of making his own arrangements. He is not the type of man who wishes to have a managing female on his hands, Alice."

"Now, there I will argue with you, Elizabeth. As Blaine is at his club, I can speak freely. All men want managing wives to organize their lives, smooth their way, manage the servants, set up the entertaining and social calendar, and keep domestic problems from them. The key is not to let them know how and when the managing is done. Blaine would not know what I was talking about, but when I am gone, he is helpless."

Elizabeth mused for a moment about her years with Reginald. Had she managed much of anything? Perhaps some of the household matters and the kitchen fare. "I see what you mean, but I assume we will have to work out those things slowly. Remember, we are not officially betrothed as yet."

"You might as well be. Everyone considers it an accomplished fact."

Elizabeth smiled and gave a little shrug. "I still do not understand how the news of our arrangement traveled so fast when we told no one but you, Blaine, Sir James, and Lady Powell. And you four declare you told no one."

Alice tossed her golden curls. "I explained how the servants gossip."

Elizabeth broadened her smile but let the subject drop. The plan was going according to their intentions, at least for the moment.

Once they sat in the theater, she felt too tired to follow the action of the play. Instead, her old doubts gushed up like the water in her spring. How much of her acquiescence to the sham betrothal could she attribute to good sense and how much to her attraction to Harry Marlowe? Since their arrangement had become known in Society, most gentlemen who previously had showered attention on her had wished her well and gracefully turned their interests elsewhere. A few had sent flowers. Sir Howell had brought her a book about castles. That part of the plan was working perfectly.

But Elizabeth's feelings about Harry only continued to grow. He drove her everywhere, had even brought his own team of horses from Suffolk so that he could take her back and forth to Richmond. Now that she and Harry had spent hours together in his well-sprung curricle, she had learned much more about him. And shared thoughts on many topics. He made her smile and laugh. He made her feel like a person of worth.

Gradually, Elizabeth had learned what had been missing from her marriage to Reginald. If he had treated her as Harry did, she would probably have loved Reginald deeply. But, however kind and generous, Reginald had always treated her as less than a full partner, as a child to be protected. Until they went to Allward, she had been satisfied in the marriage and probably could have lived all her life in that sort of shadow.

Now, just as she was poised to begin her new independent life, she questioned her reasoning. Her feelings for Harry went beyond friendship, beyond partnership in a harmless conspiracy. She dreaded giving voice to the thought, but she was afraid she was falling in love with him.

She dared not let him know. His late wife had

impeded his growth as a botanist. Elizabeth knew she could never do that, never stand in the way of his voyage.

She had no choice but to continue their charade. But she had to learn to guard her heart more carefully.

Elizabeth was not prepared for the emotions that lashed through her when the two wagonloads of furnishings arrived at Cloud Spring the next day.

Harry had been kind enough to bring her to the house to await the delivery. Now, as two burly men took down each piece and awaited her instructions, she felt a sense of sadness come over her, sadness that the life she and Reginald once had had never blossomed. She had been such an innocent when she went to Reginald's house as his bride, and she had grown but little.

When the carters carried in the Gothic sideboard, she remembered how the hideous thing frightened her the first time she saw it. With gargoyles grinning from each corner, it was atrocious indeed. She could hardly believe that she had lived with it for five years. Though it did remind her very much of several pieces at Allward in its massive ugliness.

Sally, a tin of beeswax in her hand, exclaimed over the piece. "It looks worthy of Strawberry Hill!"

"Exactly. I hate it." Elizabeth looked at Peg. "What do you think? Could you use this in the kitchen?"

Peg circled it, scratching her head. "I kinda' take to th' little toads there."

Elizabeth nodded. "Then to the kitchen it shall go. Around in back to the stairs, my good men."

Peg trotted after them to see it placed to advantage.

Sally looked amazed. "Mrs. Drayton, in the

kitchen? That looked like a valuable, not to mention fantastical, piece."

Elizabeth shrugged. "I have always despised it. I would have been happy had it fallen off the dray and smashed to pieces. But if Peg thinks she has a use for it, it can go downstairs, as long as I will not have to gaze upon it at dinnertime."

When the men unrolled carpets in the drawing room and dining room, Elizabeth had an entirely different reaction. How lovely they were in this house of light. Reginald's London house had been darker, and the colors never before glowed as they did in the brightness of her new home. Two more were placed upstairs and gave her equal pleasure in their appearance.

A sofa, however, looked worn and threadbare when in place, as did an upholstered chair. More entries for her growing list of projects, Elizabeth thought.

The men were nearly done when Harry returned. She assumed he had gone to consult with the builders on replacing the cottage roof. But before Al took the curricle to the stables, Harry carefully lifted out a large orchid.

"No home is complete without flowers, my dear."

Elizabeth thanked him profusely. "It looks so fragile, Harry. Will it not die inside?"

"It does not care for direct light. Think of it growing under the jungle canopy. But we should set it on top of a plate of wet pebbles. It likes moisture."

He carried it inside and put it on a table behind the sofa. The pale gold of dozens of tiny blossoms on the gracefully arching stem made the room come alive.

Elizabeth simply stared at it, her hand to her cheek. Tears threatened, and she could not stop them. Harry put his arm around her shoulders.

"Have you overdone things, Elizabeth? I saw you gazing into space at the theater last night. Be careful not to overtire yourself."

She laughed and wiped away the tears. "The only reason you have so much energy is that you slept through acts two and three."

"Yes, and I do not regret it for an instant. I suggest that tonight we cry off from the rout Faith has promised us to. We could have a quiet dinner at the Clarendon. Their chef is reputed to be excellent. Then, I can take you home to bed early."

"That sounds heavenly. Only another few days, and I will be able to sleep right here with no need to go back and forth to London every day."

"I often sleep at a hotel nearby when I stay late at Kew Gardens. It is just a short way from here, so while I am still helping you, I can avoid the trip to town as well."

"I do not want to inconvenience you, Harry. You have already done so much. . . ."

"And we are far from finished, unless you are tired of my phiz in your garden."

"Oh, no, I appreciate all the help . . . but I do not wish to take you away from your various experiments."

"I am having no trouble keeping up, my dear. Now, let's tackle these pictures."

Six canvases were stacked on the floor in the dining room, and several crates stood unopened in the drawing room.

Harry lifted the smallest frame out of a crate, unwrapped it, and held it up to the light. It was a watercolor she had done long ago, a simple country scene of a bridge over a winding stream in a sylvan glade.

"Did you paint this, Elizabeth?"

"Yes, many years ago, just after I left school."

"I think you showed the beginnings of a real talent. Very nice work for a young lady."

Elizabeth blanched. Though what he said was precisely the kind of comment she herself would have made, it sounded rather empty coming from him. "Faint praise?"

He looked embarrassed. "I did not mean it that way. Forgive me if my judgment was too harsh."

"Oh no, not at all harsh. Probably more praise than the work deserves." She tried to laugh away her disappointment, but she felt a little hurt deep down. She knew Harry had meant nothing unkind, but nevertheless she had to force back the sting of his words.

Harry moved the little painting aside and lifted another one from the stack, a larger canvas done in oil. It was a landscape with a windmill, probably of Dutch origin, executed in shades of brown and gray. Reginald had purchased it before they wed. It seemed too dark for this house, and she shook her head at Harry.

"I concur, Elizabeth. It is nicely done but does not fit in here. Should we send it to auction?"

"It holds no good memories for me, and I do not care much for the style."

"Then, to auction it will go."

Elizabeth drew a deep breath. To her relief, the feeling of hurt passed. She looked at the next canvas Harry held. "That one is quite dark also."

He placed it with the other items for auction and held up a still life, a scene of apples and pears in a blue dish with a white pitcher standing beside it.

Elizabeth cocked her head to one side and nodded. "I like that one. It will be perfectly suitable for the dining room."

When they finished with the paintings, she found a last crate under the table. Harry opened it and lifted out a dozen objects wrapped in yellowed paper.

Elizabeth knew exactly what they were, her old collection of china figures. She pulled the wrappings off a pitcher made in the shape of Mother Goose. "Other than my clothing, these are about the only things I brought to Reginald's household."

For the next quarter hour, Harry helped her unwrap, wash, and dry the eight little objects. She and Harry carried them upstairs and placed them on the mantel in Elizabeth's sitting room, just as she had planned.

"I guess you will think I am overly sentimental, but these do remind me of my childhood."

"And you had a happy childhood?"

"Yes, until my mother died when I was thirteen. Was your childhood happy too?"

Harry grinned broadly. "Faith and I were the tail end of a large brood. We were as wild as red Indians."

She glanced at him and saw a light in his eyes that touched at her heart. He must have been an adorable child. She had the vision of a sandy-haired tot scrambling over the rocks in a stream.

She was at a loss for words, afraid to break the spell of the moment but unwilling to push further toward unknown peril, the peril of a broken heart.

For a moment, they stood in silence then went back downstairs to the mundane task of recrating the paintings to be sent to auction.

"Do you like modern painting?" Harry slotted one canvas into the largest crate.

"Why, yes, I especially admire the work of Mr. Lawrence. His portraits are beyond compare. And Mr. Hoppner's too."

"The summer exhibition of the Royal Academy opens next week. Perhaps you would like to see it."

"Oh, yes. I would love to go." She almost bit her

tongue. She had to stop encouraging Harry to spend more time with her. But she really wanted to see the exhibition, and she had already blurted out her acceptance.

Eleven

"Elizabeth?"

When she heard Mr. Marlowe's voice, Elizabeth hastened around the house. "Good morning, Harry. Peg is hanging out the wash, and I am pulling weeds. Or at least I hope they are weeds and not flowers waiting to bloom."

She stripped off her gloves and wiped her damp hands on her apron.

He handed her a basket. "Here is something I thought you might like to have around the house."

She heard mewing and opened the lid. A tiny, pale gray kitten lifted its head and blinked in the bright light, mewing again. "Oh, it is adorable."

"I found her—if the hotel's cook is correct, she is a female—in the stable behind the hotel. The cook said she was old enough to leave her brothers and sisters."

"I shall get her a saucer of milk, and we shall see."

"Promise you will not bite off my head. I chose her for her green eyes. They reminded me of . . ." He laughed at her instant scowl.

Elizabeth tossed her head. "I choose to ignore that remark." She cuddled the tiny cat and rubbed her against her cheek. "I shall call her Misty, like the vapors that rise from the river in the early morning."

Harry caressed the kitten's ears, brushing his fingertips over Elizabeth's cheek as well.

"Now, Elizabeth, why are you pulling weeds? I have sent men to do that for you."

She peered at him over the whiskers. "I like to be part of the garden."

"I have three urns for the terrace arriving shortly. You can tell the men where to place them. But I hate to think of you hurting your beautiful hands." He leaned over and planted a kiss on the back of one and, in so doing, rubbed his nose in the kitten's soft fur.

He gave a little sneeze.

"Do you have an aversion to cats?" she asked.

"Only when my nose is tickled."

Peg brought a saucer of milk, and Misty exhibited her ability to lap it up. Elizabeth knelt on the floor and rubbed the kitten's back, laughing as the kitten arched it high while never stopping the quick slurps of her tongue.

When the clock chimed one, Elizabeth got to her feet. "I will find a length of soft wool for her to sleep on. Now, I must hurry and change. I sent Jed for Richard and Mr. Macneil some time ago. They should be here within the hour."

"I will be in the garden, seeing how Tom is doing with the climbing roses."

She hurried upstairs, giggling at how Richard would be able to pet Misty to his heart's content. Why the dowager had never allowed him to bring one of the kittens in the house was another of those mysteries about the operation of Allward she had never understood. Even when Reginald had suggested a pet for the boy, the dowager was unbending.

She paused for a moment to look at her bedchamber. Even after a week of sleeping in it, she never failed to admire the room when she stepped across the threshold. She opened the clothespress and selected an afternoon gown. What ever would she do with the evening gowns? She had not missed being away from London ballrooms for the past few nights. Alice had already found a young lady in need of a match, a girl who required Alice's considerable talents, she said. Now that Elizabeth and Harry were an accepted couple, Alice had a new mission.

Jed drove Elizabeth's gig up the drive near the stroke of two.

Richard jumped out and ran into Elizabeth's arms with an enthusiasm she had never seen in the young man before.

"Richard, my dear boy. You must be excited finally to be at Eton."

"I am just happy to be with you, Aunt Elizabeth. Grandmama does not allow me to talk of you. When I asked Mama, she said I could see you here but not to tell Grandmama."

"Your mama was right." Silently, Elizabeth praised Hester's good sense, more than she might have given the woman credit for in the past.

When he was introduced to Harry, Richard reverted to his solemn demeanor, polite and proper but showing a minimum of spirit. "How do you do, Mr. Marlowe?"

"Your aunt has told me a great deal about you."

Elizabeth found Misty and carried her to Richard. "Look what Mr. Marlowe brought me a while ago. I call her Misty."

Richard held out his hands and gently hugged the kitten. "Oh, she is beautiful."

He carried her on a tour of the house, and she fell asleep in his lap when Peg brought them gingerbread and tea in the drawing room.

Richard carefully reached over the kitten for a slice. "We never got sweets at Allward. Only at Christmas and Eastertide."

Mr. Macneil nodded. "But tell your aunt and Mr. Marlowe about your landlady."

"She is called Mrs. Jones, and she serves us cake at every evening meal."

Harry helped himself to a second square of gingerbread. "If her cake is half as delicious as Peg's, you must look forward to that."

"Well, maybe not quite this good." Richard followed Harry's example and took a second piece, as did Mr. Macneil.

"So, you like your landlady and the other boys?" Elizabeth asked.

Richard shrugged, his mouth full. Swallowing, he glanced at Mr. Macneil then took a sip of tea. Soberly he related his living arrangements, in a house with about twenty other boys, overseen by the landlady and an assistant master, Mr. Harris. Mr. Macneil had taken chambers nearby and would remain in Eton at least until Richard finished the summer term.

"The school term is called a half, Aunt Elizabeth," Richard concluded. "They have three halves. Is that not strange?"

They all laughed at the thought of a revered educational institution having divided its school year into three halves.

Harry stood and gestured to Mr. Macneil. "Might I show you the program of restoration I've begun with Mrs. Drayton's garden? I understand you and I share an interest in botany."

The two men walked through the French doors onto the terrace. Elizabeth patted the seat beside her on the sofa. When Richard sat there, they had another good, long hug.

"I have missed you, Richard. But now you are here, and whenever you can, you will be able to stay here with me. Tell me, are you making friends?"

He looked down and shook his head. "Not yet." His voice dropped even lower. "I guess nobody likes me."

Elizabeth's heart twisted in her chest. He was voicing her worst fears. "Making friends takes a long time. Just be yourself, Richard, and smile. You have such a nice smile, very special."

"But I cannot play cricket because I do not know how."

"Everyone has to learn. If you ask him, Mr. Macneil can find someone to teach you to bat."

"One of the boys said I was boasting, but I never told anyone I am an earl. They all just know it. I do not know how they found out. But I am not a braggart, Aunt Elizabeth. I am not!"

"Of course you are not."

"George said I was trying to make him feel inferior. Then he said his grandfather was an earl, and he did not believe it was anything to get excited about."

"Some of the boys will be envious of you, Richard, because you already have your title. We know that is because your father died when you were very young. To us, it was very sad, but other boys will not think about the sorrow and the loss. They could envy you for all the wrong reasons. It is sad to say, darling Richard, but other young men can be cruel and hurt your feelings on purpose."

"Why do they do that?"

"Perhaps it makes them feel important, especially when they embarrass you in front of other boys. Every one of them has been taught by their mamas that to make fun of others is wrong. But teasing makes some boys laugh. I do not know why boys delight in bringing out the worst in themselves and in others. But some of them do."

"That is what Charles does. Makes fun of me and the others laugh."

"You must be strong when other boys are unkind. Ignore them, and never make fun of anybody else, no matter what. Do you remember the Golden Rule, as your mama taught you?"

"Do not do anything to anyone you would not want to have done to you."

"Excellent, Richard. I am proud of you."

"But when I said that to Charles West, he said I was a milquetoast baby."

"Do you know what I think? I think someone once said exactly the same thing to Charles West, and it made him feel bad. So, he decided to make another person feel bad. He is probably not a bully at heart."

"Yes, he is." Richard's lower lip quivered.

"Then, let us not talk of him anymore. We will go outside to see the garden, and then I will show you a secret spring."

She wrapped an arm around his shoulders, still far too thin, and they went out through the terrace into the garden.

Harry was pointing to the arching branches of a rosebush covered with buds. "The *Rosa semperflorens* takes well to pruning. You would never know that only a week ago, we cut out dozens of old, dead branches."

Elizabeth kept her hand on Richard's back. "I want to show you the spring, but I warn you that the closer we get, the scragglier the shrubbery."

"It will take another two or three weeks to tame all this underbrush," Harry said.

They climbed the path, pushing aside the branches as they walked. Elizabeth led the way and stopped at the mouth of the grotto to let Richard go in first.

"Aunt Elizabeth! This place is like a wizard's cave. I wonder if Merlin the Magician lived here once?"

Elizabeth stepped inside after Mr. Macneil. "Perhaps he did, or at the least, one of his students. I think he must have been a very great teacher, would you not agree, Mr. Macneil?"

"Yes, indeed. One of the greatest."

For the rest of the afternoon, they talked of Merlin and King Arthur. When Jed brought the gig to take Richard and Mr. Macneil back to Eton, Richard had to break off his explanation of how Excalibur came to be in the lake.

Harry helped the boy into his seat. "You can tell me the rest of it on our next visit, Richard."

After the carriage left, Harry gave Elizabeth a big smile. "I think he is a fine lad."

"Yes, but I fear he has not yet adjusted well to the other boys." She gave him an abridged version of Richard's concerns.

"Only time will help him. But I suggest we set a day to take him into town to Astley's Amphitheater. A wonderful thing is Astley's."

"I admit to wishing I might go myself, but it was not to Alice's taste."

Harry gave a bark of laughter. "Then that settles it. I have not been for so many years I hardly remember, but this is certainly the occasion."

Harry walked through the succession houses at Kew, his head bowed in thought. No one was pressuring him to make a decision about the voyage—yet. But soon he would have to decide whether he would join the excursion or choose someone to take his place.

More and more he doubted his commitment to

the two or three years it would take to complete the journey.

His choice depended on Elizabeth, though he would not phrase it that way to her. He was prepared to pledge his life to her, but only when she was ready. Elizabeth was all he wanted in a life's companion.

Her house was perfect for them to share. He felt comfortable there and could easily build a hothouse or a conservatory or could extend the gardens—or all three. He would like to try watering some plants with that springwater to see if the minerals might affect their growth, to see if there was a difference when the water was used straight from the spring as opposed to filtering through the earth to the roots in the garden.

He enjoyed spending time with Elizabeth. They had spent the recent afternoon in her studio, attempting to draw the details of a flower. They had laughed over the difficulties of making a botanically correct picture.

He stopped and retraced his steps to the turn he had meant to take. Funny how his world had changed since he had met her. A few months ago, he had never expected to marry again. He was content in his single life, other than disliking the efforts Faith made to put him in Society. When he first met Elizabeth, he never expected his attraction to deepen into love.

The irony of the situation made him smile. His late wife's clinging ways had almost strangled him. Elizabeth was determined to maintain her fierce independence.

The longer he waited, the more likely she would be to regard him favorably. If she was happy with her independence, he would have to convince her that they could share their lives and not endanger each other's freedom of action.

He was certain she felt affection for him, but he had to bide his time for now.

"Mr. Marlowe, sir?"

He stopped abruptly and caught the eye of a young assistant.

"Mr. Michaels. What can I do for you?"

"Are we not to transplant the—"

Harry slapped his forehead. "Of course. My mind is a thousand miles distant this morning."

"Yes, sir. I've been following you. You passed our seedlings way back there." Mr. Michaels pointed down the corridor between the forests of tropical specimens.

Harry gave a bark of laughter. He had better get control of his thoughts now. There was work to be done.

Merely approaching the vicinity of Astley's Amphitheater put Richard in a festive mood. Crowds of people, many children but as many adults as well, surrounded them. Probably more than the boy had ever seen, Elizabeth thought. He grasped her hand tightly. Music filled the air as Harry bought three tickets for them.

"They promise these are the very best seats, Richard."

"Thank you, sir." He clasped his ticket tightly, eyes wide.

At the entrance, a monkey in a red coat and cap sat on the ticket taker's shoulder. "Hand yer ticket to Georgie, here, laddie."

Richard tentatively held out his ticket, and in a flash, the monkey grabbed it.

Richard gave a shout of laughter.

"'Ere, laddie. Toss this ball for 'im."

Richard tossed a red ball, and, as fast as it hit the ground, the monkey sped away and retrieved it, running on all fours, its tail curled up in the air. It scampered back and hopped to the man's waist and onto his shoulder again.

The ticket taker handed Richard the ball again, and they repeated the trick.

"Now let 'im hop up on you, laddie. Hold the ball high."

Richard extended one arm high above his head, and again, moving faster than their eyes could follow, the monkey leaped onto Richard's shoulder and stood on its hind legs, pulling the ball out of his hands.

Elizabeth watched with delight as the ticket taker, pausing to grab tickets from other attendees, put the monkey through its paces. Richard enjoyed the little brown animal so much they had to hurry to get to their seats in time for the show. Elizabeth noticed Harry hand something to the man and whisper to him before hastening to catch up with Richard and her.

The huge wooden amphitheater impressed Elizabeth, who had seen London's finest opera houses. How much more awesome must it be for Richard, who had never even attended a regional theatrical event? A gigantic chandelier of a thousand glittering cut crystals hung over the vast arena. At one end, the huge stage was curtained in red velvet. Richard gazed around the ring, his mouth gaping in wonder.

No sooner had they found their box than the orchestra played its fanfare. White horses with plumes on their bridles entered, showmen themselves, tossing their crested manes and swishing their tails as they high-stepped around the arena.

Jewels flashed brightly on their harnesses as they moved. The female riders in spangled costumes stood on the broad backs of the horses, striking poses as the horses completed circuit after circuit of the ring. A man in black tights had a foot on the back of one horse and the other foot on another's. In unison, the two horses cantered around the ring, then in smaller and smaller figure eights until the horses whirled around almost in place. Richard stood and applauded, hopping up and down, unable to stand still at the sight. He grew even more excited when the monkey, now clad in a shiny silver jacket, also performed on the back of a dapple gray pony. Georgie darted from the pony's neck to its tail and back, sitting, standing, and finally turning somersaults in the air to Richard's fervent cheers. The entire audience was on its feet.

Elizabeth found the performance breathtaking but better yet was to see Richard's excitement overflowing. His eyes were wide, and he gasped at every new feat of the strong man, the tightrope dancer, and the clowns.

At the interval, Richard was thrilled when the ticket taker joined them in the box with Georgie, who pulled a coin from behind Richard's ear, chattered at him with vigor, and accepted bits of ham from their supper tray.

When the performance was about to continue, Georgie and his master shook hands with all of them.

"I have never been so close to a monkey," Elizabeth said when they were alone again.

"I have not either." Richard was too excited to eat.

She leaned close to Harry. "I cannot thank you enough for arranging that."

He patted her hand and grinned at Richard. "Many years ago, when I was in Brazil, there was a lad aboard our ship who got a monkey. Pretty smart little fellow, it was."

"That boy was lucky," Richard said, then turned to watch the curtain rise for the Battle of the Roman Gladiators.

Two-wheeled chariots whirled around the ring at breakneck speed while men on foot banged their swords against their shields and shouted their battle cries.

Elizabeth was almost glad when it ended, for it was so realistic she worried for the safety of the performers. All managed their bows to thunderous applause.

Richard fell asleep long before Elizabeth and Harry returned him to Eton.

"The *Morning Post* said that portraits are again the order of the day." Elizabeth turned back to speak to Harry as she climbed the steps to the Royal Academy's galleries. "The *Morning Chronicle* said the present year's works excited warm and universal approbation."

Harry kept close behind her. "I doubt the term *universal* truly applies. Perhaps the writer was in the company of the artists as he made his circuit of the rooms."

Elizabeth, Harry, Faith, and Sir James joined the stream of well-dressed visitors treading the marble halls of Somerset House. Their carriages had been left below among dozens in the courtyard.

A large biblical scene by Benjamin West caught their eyes the moment they entered the first gallery.

Harry read the entry in the catalog, then peered at the canvas, his brow wrinkled. "I far prefer his great battleground scenes, as bloody as some of them are."

Mr. Turner's massive canvas was more to Sir James's taste. "Number 195, *The Decline of the Carthaginian Empire*—Rome being determined on the overthrow of her hated rival, demanded from her such terms as might either force her into war, or ruin her by compliance: the enervated Carthaginians, in their anxiety for peace, consented to give up even their arms and their children, J. W. M. Turner, R. A. . . ."

Harry arched a brow. "Quite a title even for so large a work."

Faith read the fragment of poetry that accompanied the painting.

> . . . *at Hope's delusive smile,*
> *The Chieftain's safety and the mother's pride*
> *Were to th' insidious conqu'ror's grasp resign'd;*
> *While o'er the western wave th' ensanguin'd sun,*
> *In gathering haze a stormy signal spread,*
> *And set portentous.*

Faith touched her throat and studied the painting. "That sounds very ominous."

Sir James nodded. "I believe that Turner himself wrote this poem about the surrender of Carthage."

The center of the canvas, in glowing golds and reds, showed the setting sun in a hazy storm, as the Romans' vessels landed at the quay. On either side of the picture, before the classical columns of Carthage, stood the grieving citizens, some mothers with babes in their arms, while piles of arms and booty lay in the forefront.

"Then those mothers had to give their children to the conquerors? How can such a thing of beauty be so very sad?" Elizabeth wanted to weep at the sacrifice, yet remained entranced by the gorgeous colors of Turner's sunset.

Harry took her arm. "That is a true artist, to engage one's deepest feelings."

They wandered into the next room, where suddenly Elizabeth pointed to a watercolor and exclaimed aloud, "Here is the work of my school friend 'Miss S. Stevens!' Imagine exhibiting at the Royal Academy. She is listed at Fitzroy Square. I will send her a note of congratulations."

Elizabeth remembered well that Miss Stevens's paintings were considered much less accomplished than her own when the two of them were the prize pupils in art class at Miss Prout's Academy. But that, she reminded herself, was more than twelve years ago, a dozen years in which she had not held a paintbrush. Miss Stevens had apparently pursued her talents and found success.

Faith's attention was caught by a little picture of boys playing with a kitten. "How charming this is, much more pleasant than the grieving mothers."

Elizabeth read the label. "*A Kitten Deceived* by Richard Collins." One of the boys held up a mirror before the kitten, whose arched back and hissing stare showed how clearly the tiny cat had fallen for the boys' trick. "I agree that it is easy to look at and very sweet. But the power of the Turner is unmistakable."

The four wandered among the rooms, admiring the sculpture. Frances Chantrey was the creator of a touching marble of two children that many people had stopped to admire.

"Monument to be placed in Litchfield Cathedral in memory of two only children," Harry read.

Again, Elizabeth felt a little stab of sadness. So many reminders here of the loss of children.

Sir James pointed to a dark canvas portraying a

nightmarish scene. "Now here is a strange one. Henry Fuseli, *Theodore in the Haunted Wood, deferred from rescuing a female chased by an Infernal Knight.*"

The mysterious forest gave her a shiver. "I find the portraits much more comfortable. There is a wonderful likeness of Her Royal Highness the Duchess of Gloucester by Sir Thomas Lawrence. And the landscapes and the nature sketches."

"Or the architectural drawings." Harry pointed his catalog at a sketch for a national monument to commemorate the victories of Waterloo and Trafalgar. "Mr. Soane is not only a great teacher."

As they went back down the staircase, Elizabeth pondered the wide range of emotions she had felt in the last two hours. More than anything, she felt a kinship to those mothers of Carthage.

Once she and Harry sat again in Harry's curricle, the traffic in The Strand seemed heavier than usual. It seemed to add to Elizabeth's sense of melancholy.

Harry gave her a close look. "I take it from your reaction to some of those pieces of artwork that you care deeply for children. Forgive me for raising a sensitive subject, my dear."

She nodded. "That is all right, Harry."

"You need not answer, for it is really not a subject I should even mention. But you were married for nine years and had no children."

Elizabeth sat still for a moment while Harry maneuvered the carriage around a dray loaded with barrels. When they were moving more freely again, she gave a little sigh.

"I hoped for children, at least at the beginning of our marriage. But later, when we were at Allward, I began to be glad I did not have to raise a child in that atmosphere. I hope it has not marked Richard forever."

"Caroline thought her illness was due to the loss of

a child, but the doctors explained to me it was only an aberration of her mind. Though she told her mother and several others that she was increasing, the doctor said she never actually was."

How awful it must have been for both of them. "Poor soul."

"Yes, she was."

Elizabeth settled back in her seat. She knew it was not too late for her to bear a child. Many women nine and twenty, and much older, had babies. She stole a look at Harry. He would make a wonderful father. But he was bound for Brazil and far beyond. Never would she ask him to give up a voyage he yearned to take. Despite the fact she sometimes forgot, their arrangement was strictly temporary. Sadly so.

Twelve

In the post a few days later, a letter arrived from Miss Stevens.

Elizabeth carried it to the garden and sat on a bench opposite the budding rosebush. How nice of—wait, it came from Serena Stevens, not her friend Sarah. She unfolded it quickly.

In flowing script, Elizabeth's old school friend reported her change of name, from the familiar *Sarah* to the more memorable *Serena.*

Elizabeth had written about her marriage, her years in Yorkshire, her loss of Reginald, and her move to London, without giving many details. Serena replied that she certainly remembered Elizabeth and thanked her for her kind comments on her work at the Royal Academy exhibition.

The message went on to invite Elizabeth to a "little gathering of artists and friends" at Serena's home in Fitzroy Square in three days. "Please bring a companion or two if you wish. I adore a crush."

A party at her old friend's home? An artist's home? Even though she had promised herself to forgo most London gatherings, this just might be an interesting change from what had become the usual, and Harry might enjoy the novelty. Since she had taken up residence at Cloud Spring, Harry had continued to help her with so many things, she needed a way to repay him. He often stayed at the little hotel in

Richmond and spent half the day in her garden, half at Kew.

There were few late nights in the carriage and no more kisses, thankfully. She was much too vulnerable to the delight of his caresses to dare kissing him again.

She glanced again at Serena's letter. When she next saw Harry, she would see if he was amenable to her plan.

Early the next day, Harry brought another carpenter to look at the proposed addition of a conservatory to the house. When they were finished talking, she invited Harry for a cup of tea.

Peg brought the tea tray as Elizabeth and Harry sat in the drawing room before a glowing fire.

"Even in May, there is still a chill in the air, especially in the morning," Harry said.

"The fire feels good."

He looked around and nodded. "This room is looking very settled, as if you had been here for years, instead of just a few weeks."

"I agree. And my bedchamber is looking almost finished. But there are still many things to arrange. And a few to buy."

"When is the auction? Would you care to go and watch your paintings be sold?"

"Do you think it would be wise? What if I get upset if a picture does not reach a good price?"

"Or more likely exclaim with joy when the bid exceeds your expectations?"

"I shall think about it. But I have another engagement you might enjoy." She handed the note to him.

He read it and handed it back. "I think it might be a most interesting change from our usual kind of amusements. Are you planning to stay at Alice's that night?"

"I suppose I should in case it runs late."

* * *

Alice was only too happy to have Elizabeth stay, making Elizabeth promise to remember every detail and give her a full account the next day.

At Elizabeth's first sight of Serena's house in Fitzroy Square, she thought it quite ordinary, nothing distinctive at all. But inside was a different story.

After she and Harry left their things in the small room at the front of the house, they went into a large room, two-stories high, lit with pink lanterns. A haze of smoke hung over the room. Dozens of people, all talking and laughing at once, filled every corner. A few were garbed as she and Harry were, in evening dress. Most looked far less formal, but colorfully so.

Elizabeth felt as though she had stepped into an oriental bazaar. Many ladies wore loose garments of bright cerulean blue, turquoise, crimson, and orange festooned with fringe. Some men wore loose vests or jerkins covered with silvery spangles and sparkling gems.

Harry whispered in Elizabeth's ear. "I did not know it was a masquerade. Or perhaps we have wandered into the costume warehouse at Astley's."

A man who looked like Elizabeth's idea of how a pirate would appear grabbed her hand and led her deeper into the chaos.

"Dance with me, Princess." His voice and his fake Spanish accent went right along with the pirate role.

Musicians struck up outside in the garden, and people responded, moving to the music, though it was nothing like the dancing Elizabeth had ever seen. More like what she would have expected at a village fete after a number of barrels of ale had been consumed.

But as Mr. Pirate led her through the crowd,

weaving back and forth, she began to think there might be a pattern she could discern. The music ended abruptly, and he caught her in his arms and placed a wet smack on her cheek. "My beautiful princess, I have abducted you, and I now wish to carry you off and ravish you."

Before Elizabeth could think how to react to such an outrageous statement, she recognized Serena even with hair as orange as fire and eyes outlined in charcoal.

Serena spotted her at the same moment. "Elizabeth! Elizabeth! My dear."

Serena rushed to embrace her, and they held each other at arm's length, looking at what a dozen years had done. "I would have known you anywhere, Lizzie."

"And I would have known you, Serena, except . . . except for your hair."

"Someday I will tell you all about my metamorphosis, dear." Serena gave a shove to the hovering pirate. "Go bother someone else, John, this is my old school friend."

The pirate shrugged and melted into the crowd.

"Do not pay any mind to him, Lizzie. He is quite harmless, but he loves to act ridiculous. He might be the least obnoxious of my suitors."

Elizabeth saw Harry holding two glasses of champagne and called to him. "Harry, over here."

Astonishment glimmered on his face for a moment when he saw her companion, but by the time he strode to them, he was all that was polite.

"Serena, may I present to you Mr. Harry Marlowe?"

Instead of making a little curtsy, Serena took one of the goblets from him and drained it in two gulps. "Thank you, Harry, you are precisely what I need. The man with champagne."

He bowed, offering her the other glass. "If you are particularly thirsty, Miss Stevens, I shall immediately go for more."

"How adorable you are," Serena said, running her left hand up and down his arm while taking the second glass with her right. She took a sip. "Mmmm. Delicious. Is it not wonderful that we can have French wine now without having to pay a premium to the smugglers?"

Elizabeth watched, trying not to look like a sun-struck ninny. She felt her eyes might jump out of her head at Serena's behavior, more like what she would expect from a tavern wench than someone who had attended Miss Prout's Academy.

Harry went off to fetch more champagne and as Serena was surrounded by friends, Elizabeth let herself drift into the crowd, keeping Serena in sight but staying out of the way.

Elizabeth hoped she did not look shocked as she let her glance rove back and forth over the people. Several women smoked little cigars, not a sight one would encounter at a ton rout. The dancing was distinctly odd, the apparel more suited to a gypsy camp. It had a certain allure. A part of the world she had never before encountered. The fascination of the forbidden?

Elizabeth was relieved she had not given in to her temptations to ask Alice and Blaine to come along. They had more than hinted, but though Alice might have enjoyed herself, she would have gossiped about it for weeks. Although, Elizabeth reminded herself, that would not be so bad. Alice might stop relating every detail she could wring out of Elizabeth to all her friends if she had a new topic. Alice did not mean anything harmful, she simply could not stop talking. And talking. And talking.

Elizabeth noticed Harry return to Serena's side

with a whole tray of brimming champagne glasses. Serena took one with a smile at Harry, just a quick smile, but it was followed by another look, almost of surprise. As Elizabeth watched, she could almost read the change on Serena's face from a noncommittal casual smile . . . to a wink of interest . . . to a seductive grin that left no doubt Serena found Harry a most attractive man. A stab of anger brought Elizabeth a shiver, and she suddenly felt very thirsty herself.

She moved around a woman in violet, a man in a rainbow coat, and to Harry, looking dignified in deepest midnight blue. His eyes were glued to Serena, and Elizabeth fought off another surge of envy. What had come over her? Their entire friendship—or whatever it might be called—was based on a tenuous agreement that had no real substance. Instead, it was an out and out falsehood. She had no right to expect him to pay attention to her in a crowd of strangers.

Why should he not interest himself in Serena? Even the most malicious person would have to admit the lady had many man-attracting qualities. Sultry eyes, full lips, a voluptuous figure wrapped in diaphanous scarves that sometimes revealed as much as they covered.

Elizabeth moved next to Harry and took a champagne goblet. He did not even notice. His eyes were on Serena. Peeling away those layers, she imagined.

Again, she stepped back and let herself disappear into the crowd. She took a deep swallow of the champagne, angry at herself for such a foolish snit. *Admit it, Elizabeth, you are jealous when you have no right to be. And you are not being honest with yourself. You might be awestruck too if some handsome man had teased you with a smile rather than a pirate's leer.*

Back inside Serena's studio, Elizabeth saw a few

paintings on the wall and others on easels, as if put out for show. But no one was looking at the moment. Elizabeth took the opportunity to see just how good her old friend Sarah-Serena had become. Even in the flickering light, Elizabeth had to admit the paintings were accomplished in technique. She leaned closer, seeing how the artist had let the color flow onto the paper with fluid strokes. Elizabeth would have to remember this the next time she picked up her brushes.

"Here you are!" Serena's voice interrupted her study of the canvases.

Serena was plastered against Harry's side, one arm entwined with his, the other holding a half-filled goblet.

"Miss Stevens has been telling me all about your years together in school."

Elizabeth almost choked on another sip of champagne. "Serena, I cannot believe you have been boring Harry with such lackluster tales."

"Oh, we have talked of a few other things, too." Serena turned her face up to his and grinned, fluttering her eyelashes preposterously. If she had been a tonnish young miss at some Mayfair ball, he would have sniggered at her obviousness.

Instead, he looked tongue-tied and wide-eyed. Elizabeth wished she could tell him how silly he looked. She waved at the pictures. "I am very impressed, Serena. Your work with oils is excellent, and the flowers are particularly good."

"I submitted several oils to the Academy, but they accepted only the watercolor. I am sure they have a limit on how many female oil painters they will allow."

"But how can they—"

"Oh, they can, do you not agree, Harry?"

Elizabeth clenched her teeth and tried not to

shudder as he smiled at Serena and shook his head.
A lock of hair fell over his forehead, and Serena
brushed it back, her hand lingering, it seemed to
Elizabeth, for an excessively long time.

"I was telling Miss Stevens about your house, Elizabeth."

"Yes, Lizzie, how lucky you are to have found
what Harry describes as a perfect spot."

Elizabeth blanched. Serena had known him just
an hour, and she called him by his given name.

Serena spoke to Elizabeth, but she gazed at
Harry. Adoringly. "May I come someday with my
sketch pad?"

Elizabeth forced a smile. "Why, of course, Serena.
Whenever you wish."

"Harry says you are painting again. I hope you
have learned to be a little looser." She gave Harry
another broad grin. "Looser in everything you do.
Once I got away from Miss Prout's, I had to relearn
all my techniques." She gave another giggle. "I
know, Lizzie, this is not quite your kind of group,
but if you would loosen up, even tonight, you might
have a good time."

At first Elizabeth boiled inside. How dare Serena
say such a thing? But, on second thought, Elizabeth
had to admit it was true. She definitely felt out of
place, and she imagined her lips were primly
pursed, just like the dowager's. The thought made
Elizabeth shudder.

Nothing was going on here that she had not seen
before. Why act as though she was as stuffy as an old
maid? Had she not whirled around the terrace with
a pirate already? And why had she not enjoyed it?

For a moment, she paused to listen to a pair of
men arguing about the very painting by Turner she
had agonized over at the Royal Academy.

"He is breaking new ground with his skies," one said.

"No," the other insisted. "He is just a swindler, dressing up his canvases with bright colors to stun the eye."

Elizabeth held up a hand. "Could there be another explanation? Could Turner not be accentuating the contrasts?"

The older of the two men shrugged. "How so?"

"The dark sections of the painting show the agony of the mothers of Carthage, and the very beauty of the bright sunset makes their anguish more incisive."

"Exactly," the first man declared. "A gifted analysis."

The older man was not finished. "But the way Turner lays on the paint . . ."

Elizabeth chuckled to herself and moved on, leaving the debaters behind.

"Are you lonely or sad?" another young man asked, pushing through the crowd to her side.

"Why, neither. Do I look upset?" she replied with a grin, letting a bit of flirtation enter her tone.

"A bit. I prescribe a little music and dancing to preserve your smile."

"My smile?"

"I saw you when you entered. You had the most enchanting smile. . . ." He reached for her hand, and she let him pull her between the earnest debaters toward the dancing.

He wore a threadbare green coat over an open-necked shirt with a red kerchief around his neck.

The music was a sort of waltz, though the couples on the terrace were moving in all sorts of patterns she had never seen. If Harry could fall under the spell of Serena Stevens, she supposed she had the right to do a little dancing, if that was what one called the kind of energetic shuffling they had begun, rocking from one side to another and hardly moving in the press of dancers around them.

She wanted to ask what the dance was called, but she did not even know the name of the young man. Had she ever before danced with a man to whom she had not been formally introduced?

As if he knew her thoughts, he grabbed her hands and spun her around. "I am Rowley, Peter Rowley."

She gasped for breath and grinned back. "I am Elizabeth, but you may as well call me Lizzie, as Serena does."

"Serena? You mean our hostess?"

Elizabeth nodded.

"I have never met her. I came with some other fellows. I think one of them knows her."

For some reason, this put Elizabeth into whoops of laughter.

Toward noon, Elizabeth arose, feeling very much the effects of last night's overindulgence. Harry would be even more miserable, she figured. She had been short with him when he brought her back to Alice's house, but would he remember?

She swallowed two doses of headache powder before she could dress. Both she and Harry had been foolish last night. They should not have had so much champagne. Harry had stared at Serena all night. But had she been any better?

Elizabeth squeezed her eyes shut as she thought of the men she had flirted with. And how she had danced with abandon.

Alice sat in ambush in the morning room, eager for conversation. After a cup of strong coffee, Elizabeth pretended she felt fine. She decided on the same theme she had taken with Harry last night. "Other than the attire of the guests and the setting in Serena's studio, it was not much different than any party you and I have attended in the last months."

Alice gestured dismissively. "Oh, come now, that seems unlikely."

Elizabeth described the garments worn by several guests and the crowd on the dance floor doing a semblance of a waltz. "Many of them were arguing about the abilities of various artists, and others were gossiping. Except that I did not know the persons about whom they spoke, it was just like listening to the chatter at any ball."

"But I thought they would do all sorts of shocking things."

"One woman said her slippers pinched her feet and so she took them off and went barefoot. Is that shocking enough for you?" Elizabeth decided not to mention the little cigars. Alice might want to try one.

"If you will drive me out to Richmond, Alice, I will show you how the garden is progressing."

"Is Harry not coming to drive you?"

"I could send him a note and save him the trouble if you want a little jaunt. He said he might have a meeting to go to later here in Town, so he will welcome the reprieve." Elizabeth found the fibs tripped lightly off her tongue. When all of this was over, she would have to be sure she stuck closely to the truth for the rest of her life. Otherwise, she faced the future as an accomplished liar.

Alice could not resist a longer time for her quiz. "If you tell me more details about the party. And if we can stop at that little shop you told me about in the village, I could use an afternoon taking the air."

Elizabeth made sure her note to Harry was simple and innocuous, without a mention of the coolness she had felt last night. She did not want to burden him with her petty thoughts. In another day or two, she would put them behind her.

The source of her disquiet, she told herself, was simply the surprise. After weeks of having all of Harry's kind regard, she had been stunned to have his attention go to someone else. If she was not attached to Harry in any permanent way, she could not expect him to pay her exclusive attention, especially when they were away from the very people they were trying to delude.

There was one more major hurdle in their path, the week at Daveny Manor. Why they had agreed to the house party, she could not imagine. Once that was over, the Season was nearly finished for another year. But next year at this time, no one would give her a second thought. Harry would be gone away, and she could enjoy her freedom.

Thirteen

Harry gazed out through the glass wall of Faith's conservatory at the darkening sky. He had not seen Elizabeth for two days, since the evening of the party at her artist friend's. He told himself the hostile undercurrent he felt in her good night had to be his imagination. Surely she could not have felt discomfort at his mild attraction to Miss Stevens. Elizabeth was not that sensitive.

Or was she? Perhaps she felt as out of place as he had at the gathering, unsure of how to behave in such a setting. But once he had determined that no one was paying the slightest attention to him, he had quite enjoyed the company of the unique Miss Stevens. And her guests.

If Elizabeth had been quiet on the way back to Alice's house, he had attributed it to the exhaustion brought on by what the company had called dancing and the eventual effects of multiple glasses of wine.

Surely Elizabeth had not felt envy of Serena Stevens. Though Serena appeared to have the very thing Elizabeth was struggling to achieve, independence.

In just a few days, he and Elizabeth would leave for the Daveny's house party in Sussex. He did not remember why they promised to attend, but Alice and Blaine would be there. He supposed it would be endurable. Perhaps there were some interesting gardens to explore. One thing he promised himself: no trips into Brighton to see the Prince Regent's monstrosity. The old reprobate was remodeling the pavilion again, or so Harry had heard. More wasteful expense to the public purse.

He untangled his cotton wicks, part of his system to water each of his fledgling plants in Faith's conservatory. With one end in a bucket of water and the other in the soil, the wicks would keep the little shoots watered. Just as long as Faith's butler kept the buckets full.

A little more than a week later, Harry almost regretted the end of their stay at the Daveny's.

Lazy afternoons walking with Elizabeth among the butterflies in the garden. Watching her sketch with the other ladies. Listening to her speak of her growing homesickness for Cloud Spring.

The only blot on their good time had been their stop at Eton on the way to Daveny Manor. Richard had been glum, and Elizabeth worried about him. As she had feared, he had not made friends easily, and Eton boys had a way of being hard on new students. But she seemed to put her concerns behind her as the week progressed.

There had been a few men-only hours of fishing and two sessions on the archery range. For the most part, however, he had stayed at Elizabeth's side. Or across a whist table. Or turning the pages as she played the fortepiano.

Even the most jaded observer, he was certain, would have acknowledged him as the most attentive of husbands-to-be.

Which is exactly how he wanted to be seen by the Davenys and their guests. And how he wished to be regarded by Elizabeth.

On their last evening, they left the tea table to walk in the warm darkness on the lawn.

Elizabeth wore a white gown that almost glowed. "I never asked you what you thought of Serena, Harry."

He chose his words carefully. "I think she is a talented artist. An unusual female. In fact, I think she glories in her unconventional behavior."

"Yes, I am sure she does. I think she was very interested in you."

"Nonsense. All we talked about was you."

"Now it is my turn to say 'nonsense.'"

The slender crescent of the moon did not obscure the canopy of stars.

They strolled toward the bower at the end of the garden where a little bench stood under the arch of rose-covered branches. The scent was strong in the still air.

"Your garden will look much like this in another month or two."

"I hope it has the same fragrance. This is intoxicating."

Harry drew her down beside him. All week he had yearned to kiss her, to caress her, to awaken again that hint of passion he had felt on the night they had agreed to their sham betrothal.

But he had hesitated until now. He had to take care. He did not wish to push her toward making their bargain a real one until he knew that she felt she had achieved her goal of independence. He could not decide whether to tell her he was giving up the idea of the voyage. So, he had vacillated, one day deciding to be straightforward, the next thinking that he should move more cautiously.

Now as they pressed together, and she leaned a little on his shoulder, the words simply escaped him.

He tilted her chin up and lightly touched her

lips. He felt her breath quicken as he rubbed his thumb along her soft cheek.

How was it he planned to ask her? What were those convincing arguments he had devised? His brain seemed empty.

He slipped his arm around her back and molded her to him. She yielded easily, wrapping her arms around his neck.

She murmured something, perhaps only his name, but he gloried in the sound of it, a little wild, a little crazy.

He looked into her eyes, then gave himself to the kiss, deep and throbbing, making every corner of his body answer to his passion.

This was not a moment for conversation, but a time of pure sensation unfettered by conditions or qualifications.

Elizabeth trembled against Harry's chest. She was afire, burning to the depths of her being. His lips caressed her cheek like little feathers, then found her mouth again with a gentle ferocity that threatened her control. Storms rippled through her, stealing her breath, fogging her mind, and dizzying her senses.

She clasped him tighter and curled her fingers into his hair. She wanted to tell him they must end their pretend betrothal, that she wanted it to be real, that she would wait for his return. "Harry?"

The sound of tinkling laughter invaded her consciousness. She could feel a different tension in Harry's shoulders.

Alice's voice was barely audible. "Do not disturb them. Perhaps they will finally admit . . ." The retreating footsteps faded away.

Elizabeth pulled away slowly and brushed back her hair. "I fear we had an audience." The moment had passed, and she no longer knew what to say.

His arms fell away. "I wonder how long they were watching."

She took a deep breath. "It does not matter. But I think I got a little carried away—"

"As did I," he said quickly.

She rearranged her shawl. "No real harm done, I suppose."

He nodded, trying to revive his crushed cravat.

"Let me help you." She smoothed out some of the creases and pinched others back into place.

"Thank you."

She stood. "I think we should go back now, before . . . before . . ."

"Before they depend too much on their imaginations."

Elizabeth started walking, and he matched her steps. "I have been thinking about stopping at Eton tomorrow on our way back to Richmond. I suspect Richard would be glad to see us, but I do not want him to feel I am hovering, worrying too much. He needs to develop his self-reliance. Perhaps it is better if we stay away for a while."

"Yes, I am sure you are correct."

She walked a little faster once the house was in sight. "We will leave about ten?"

"Yes, that should put us back in good time."

She was almost running by the time she reached the steps. "Then I will see you at breakfast." Before he could take her in his arms again, she hastened into the house and sped to her bedchamber.

A single candle flickered on the dressing table. Even in the dimness, her cheeks looked raw, her lips swollen. Another five minutes and things could have gotten out of hand.

Why had she pretended to be compliant in this sham betrothal? Now, she was the victim instead of the perpetrator of the hoax. For as surely as she stood here before the mirror, her nerves still singing from his embrace, she had fallen in love with Harry Marlowe.

Elizabeth looked at a pile of strange books in her library. Haunting the bookshops was a pleasure she was saving for after Harry's departure. It was little enough compensation for losing his companionship, but at least it would give her something to look forward to.

Sally carried another canvas bag loaded with books. "While you were away, I thought of all Father's books and decided to bring some of them to you."

"Whatever could you be thinking?" Elizabeth asked.

"Mama has been after Father to clear out some of the books in his library. He has volumes spilling out of his bookshelves and stacked all over the floor, everything from Herodotus and Homer to Hannah More. I simply cleared a shelf and brought them to you."

"What will he say when he finds them missing?"

"I told him I was taking some, and he agreed. If he ever wants one of them back, he knows where they are. I am solving his problem and helping you at the same time."

"As long as your father agrees, I am delighted."

Sally lugged the bag into the library and plopped it on the floor, reaching in and handing a few volumes to Elizabeth.

"Just tell me what others you want, and I will look for them."

"Oh, I could not impose upon you like that."

"I love doing it. And Father receives at least three or four new books every week, sometimes more. I think he has more on the floor than on the shelves."

Elizabeth looked at the titles she held. *Poems of Lovelace, Cicero's Orations.* One she did not mention aloud, wondering how in the world a copy of Boccaccio's *Decameron* came from a parson's collection.

Sally picked up three more. *Canterbury Tales* and two volumes of Goldsmith's *History of England.* What were we looking for on Tuesday? I could not remember the name."

"Virgil. *The Aeneid.*"

"Oh, yes. If Mr. Cooper cannot find it, I'll search for it."

When Sally danced off, Elizabeth sat at the table and listed each book in Sally's pile, then copied the inventory to give to Sally's father. Mr. Iveson was a kindly man who had called on her a few days before, welcoming her to the parish. She looked forward to visiting the vicarage and meeting Sally's mother.

Just as she was writing the last title, Peg knocked on the open door.

"Mrs. Drayton, a lady and a gentleman . . . or I should say two persons have called . . . Miss Stevens and Mr. Rowley."

"Oh, yes, Peg. Please take them to the drawing room and then bring us a tea tray." Elizabeth could have laughed out loud at the look of puzzlement on Peg's face, though whether it was over the color of Serena's hair or the outfit she was wearing, it was hard to tell.

Elizabeth brushed off her hands and took off her apron, trying to brush up her flyaway strands of hair escaping from the bun and tuck them under her cap. On second thought, she took off the cap and pulled the pins out of her hair, shaking it down and free. She had a momentary vision of the dowager's stern visage, quickly replaced by the laughter of Harry Marlowe.

Combing it with her fingers, she fanned out her hair and headed for the drawing room.

"Why, Serena, how nice to see you. And Peter, I am delighted. But I thought you did not know Miss Stevens."

Serena laughed. "He does now. He came to me to find *you*, Lizzie."

Serena stood before the painting over the mantel. "This is good, Lizzie. Where did it come from?"

"My late husband had it before I married him."

"Who painted it? Do you have more?"

"No, none of that artist's work. I do not remember his name. Obviously, he was Dutch."

"Pity. It looks quite valuable. Tell me why you decided to move out here to Richmond."

Elizabeth felt Peter's gaze on her as she gave her reasons.

"But what of your delicious friend Harry? He told me he lived in Mayfair. Why do you want to be so far away? Do you two not have some sort of agreement?"

Elizabeth did not know what to say. All the pat little phrases she and Harry had devised to obfuscate the truth seemed inadequate.

Peter interrupted. "I came because I wanted to see you again, Lizzie."

Serena threw him an amused look. "He was quite insistent."

"I was. I am a beginning painter, and I wish to paint you, Lizzie. You are the perfect model for me."

Elizabeth had visions of the nude sketches tacked on Serena's walls. That she would not do.

"Are you hoping to make your mark with portraits?"

"Yes, I believe I have promise, so my instructors have told me."

Elizabeth could imagine no problem. "Why, yes. I believe I can spare a few hours for you."

"If you do not like my sketches, I will not press on, Lizzie."

Serena patted Elizabeth's arm. "You may become famous as the model who inspired the latest genius."

Elizabeth felt flattered, but as she showed her guests around the house and up to the spring, she thought more of how she could answer Serena's question about Harry and her.

She had come to no conclusion when the pair of artists climbed into their gig for the return trip to Fitzroy Square.

Serena leaned down and touched Elizabeth's flyaway hair. "Loose, Lizzie. It looks very good loose. But you never answered my question about Harry. Are you going to marry him?"

For the first time, Elizabeth spoke her wish out loud. "I hope to."

Serena lifted her hands in a despairing motion. "My rotten luck."

As they waved from the bottom of the hill, Elizabeth could not believe she had said those words.

Fourteen

Two days later as Elizabeth posed for Peter in the drawing room, she could not stop thinking of the numerous things she should be doing instead of trying to stay motionless while he drew her. She tried counting to a thousand but never got past sixty. She could not seem to rid her mind of her concerns about Richard. And when she snuck a glance at Peter, he was sometimes just staring at her, hardly moving his pencil at all.

She heard voices outside but not what was being said. Abruptly, Mr. Macneil rushed into the room, shoving Peg out of the way. His face was red, and he was panting from his exertion. "Forgive me, Mrs. Drayton, but is Richard here?"

"Why, no. Not since last week when you both—"

"Oh, no! Then he has disappeared!"

Fear shot through her like a dagger. "Disappeared? What do you mean?"

"He is gone. No one has seen him for two days."

"But how could that happen?"

"I do not know. I left Eton the day before yesterday. He knew I would not be around until today. I spent time with Mr. Marlowe at Kew, then went into London and stayed with a friend. When I returned to Mrs. Jones's house this morning, he was not there. Everyone said they thought he was with me. But he was not, Mrs. Drayton, and now I am afraid he is gone. It is all my fault."

"Is he not staying with some friend?" A dull ache of dread filled her chest and clogged her thoughts.

"No one thinks so. He knows so few of the boys, just those at his house. I asked his Latin tutor, and he has not seen Richard for several days."

"Where could he have gone?"

Mr. Macneil turned his hat round and round in his hands. "I do not know. I was hoping he had come here."

Peter put down his chalk and wiped his hands on his pants. "Who is missing?"

Elizabeth paced the room, twisting her fingers together. "Richard is my nephew, Peter. He is only nine."

"Poor lad. Who else does he know in London?"

"No one, not even my cousins have met him yet. Though he could have their direction."

"I will go there at once," Mr. Macneil said, his voice unsteady.

"Wait a moment. Perhaps there are other possibilities. Peg, would you be kind enough to bring Mr. Macneil a drink of water? Please sit down, Owen."

He obeyed readily, dropping his head into his hands.

Elizabeth tried to think, but she had terrible visions of highwaymen and thieves and the men who used young boys for dangerous jobs, like the chimney sweep, boys being captured by press-gangs and shipped off forever. Richard was not safe alone.

"Have you notified the school authorities, Mr. Macneil?"

"No, I hoped he would have come to you."

She turned to the artist, who sat quietly, lost in thought. "Peter, can you please do me a favor?"

"I should like to help in any way I can."

"If you could take a note to my cousin in Brook Street immediately, I would be most grateful. Mr. Macneil, I suggest you return to Eton, notify the authorities, and begin a search of the school and the town. You may take my cob. I have only ridden him once, but he seems an easy goer."

Both young men agreed, and Elizabeth sat down at her desk to write notes to Alice and Hester. She longed to write to Harry, but after all he had done for her in the last weeks, she hesitated to embroil him in such an affair. At least not yet. Perhaps Richard was just off sulking. Yet, down deep, she knew it was more than that.

Mr. Macneil's haggard face managed a tiny grin. "He still may come here, Mrs. Drayton. If he walked, it might take him a long time. Especially if he tried to follow the river."

Elizabeth nodded, trying to visualize the twists of the Thames between Eton and Richmond. "I hope you are right. I will send you a message at your rooms if he arrives. In the meantime, perhaps he will come back of his own accord."

Peter boxed up his pencils and brushes. "I will take your letter as soon as it is ready."

"Thank you." Elizabeth wrote a quick note to Alice asking for her to look out for Richard and gave it to Peter.

Mr. Macneil, refreshed by the drink, expressed his remorse.

Elizabeth made a gesture of dismissal. "If there is any blame, I share it with you. I pushed for Richard to come to Eton, as you know. I should have known his lack of contact with other boys would make it very difficult for him. When I talked to him just a few days ago, I saw his discomfort, his lack of enthusiasm. I should have seen how upset he was. For a sensitive child in his position, I should have seen to it that the school gave him special assistance. I failed him."

"But he was my responsibility, and I was gone when he most needed me."

When both men were gone, Elizabeth allowed her tears to fall. Why had they not been more understanding at Eton, smoothed the way for a boy so new to the school? But it was not the fault of school officials. If his mother and the dowager had only treated him like a normal boy and let him have friends and playmates . . . But none of that mattered now. He simply had to be found.

Elizabeth struggled to compose a letter to Hester. There was no need to alarm her unnecessarily. Nor could Hester do much from so far away. But if their situations had been reversed, Elizabeth would want to have been informed. Carefully she constructed her sentences to minimize the sound of danger, though she could not deny that the message was very frightening. When she could make no further improvements, she folded and sealed it and sent it off.

She hardly dared to imagine what expressions of terror would greet her message. Hester would be frantic, as would the dowager. Exactly the same as Elizabeth felt this moment.

Now, the hours stretched before her in agony. She paced, she worried her lip until she had to check the mirror to be sure it was not bleeding. She spread some salve to help her stop the tendency and took to twisting and retwisting her hair until her fingers ached.

To ease the concern of Peg, who hovered over her with endless cups of tea, Elizabeth tramped through the gardens and the orchards, never more than a call away from the house.

Later, Sally arrived with a basket of fresh buns, saying Peg's sister had told her to come quickly.

Elizabeth told Sally about Richard's disappearance but said that she had no appetite.

Sally sympathized but insisted Elizabeth have a cup of tea and a bun. "You need to stay strong, Mrs. Drayton. Now is not the time to stop eating."

"I promise not to indulge in hysterics, my dear."

"You must keep talking about Richard. Somewhere in your thoughts there might be a clue to where he could have gone."

"I cannot help but dwell on his upbringing. His mother does not try to defy the dowager, whose ideas are too strict. She is a tyrant."

Sally urged her to take a bun. "Does Mr. Marlowe know?"

"No, I did not send him a message. Perhaps I should have."

"He would know how to organize a search."

Absently, Elizabeth took a bite of the bun, hardly tasting it. "But he is a busy man. He has already done so much for me, I hesitate—"

"Mrs. Drayton! He will want to help. I have never known a more charitable and supportive gentleman."

"You are right, Sally. I will send for Harry."

Not a quarter hour later, Harry rode up the drive.

She rushed out of the house.

He slid down from the saddle. "What is the matter? You look upset—"

"Oh, Harry, Richard is missing. I fear he has run away!"

He dropped the reins and took her in his arms, rocking her. "What? Run away?"

She explained everything, fighting back more tears.

Harry caressed her shoulders. "I will do all I can to help. Now, is there anything he did last week that might help us figure out what he was thinking? Was there anything he said?"

She led him to the drawing room, and they sat down, his face as serious as hers.

"I have racked my brain since the moment Mr. Macneil brought the news. So far, I have thought of nothing that hints at what he might have done. I hope that Mr. Macneil overreacted and that Richard has been found at Eton, simply hiding in a corner where no one has yet looked."

Harry tented his fingers and tapped them together. "I concur. That is by far the most likely explanation. But in case it does not work out that way, every moment we spend thinking of what he might have done is well spent."

"Yes, if he ran away, he must have had some goal, some end in mind. I cannot believe he would have tried to go back to Allward, for he was so glad to be away. Although, he could miss his mother and grandmother very much."

"If he was thinking clearly, he could have simply written to them and they would have immediately sent the carriage for him."

"That is true."

"It is more likely that he would come here, to you, Elizabeth. He is fond of you and knows you have a soft heart. If he has been bullied by other boys—"

"I pray that is not the case." She gave a mournful look. "Though I admit it is the probable cause."

"Let us ask Sally to stay here for the rest of the afternoon in case he shows up, and we will go to Eton and question some of the boys."

"I am quite certain we will pass Mr. Macneil on the road."

"Then we will take the most obvious roads and hope to see him."

But they did not meet Mr. Macneil until they arrived at the house where Richard boarded. Mrs. Jones, the landlady, was in tears, unable to string together an intelligible apology.

All twenty of the boys sat in the dining room, many with heads bowed and casting guilty looks at one another.

Mr. Macneil took Elizabeth and Harry aside. "Mrs. Jones is overset and useless for the moment. She cannot even say Richard's name without wringing her hands and crying, 'the little earl, the little earl.' She took her responsibilities toward him very seriously, and apparently she has a letter from his mother insisting that Mrs. Jones treat him with the strictest hand. There is a prescribed schedule he is supposed to follow and a volume of—"

"Of the dowager's improving tracts," Elizabeth finished his sentence. "I am sure the dowager dictated that letter to Hester. Poor Richard. Did Mrs. Jones maintain that schedule?"

"I assume she tried, but . . . For the moment, she is unable to be of much assistance. One of the assistant masters, Mr. Harris, who lives here too, and I have questioned the boys," Mr. Macneil said. "They claim no special knowledge of problems. None of them seem to claim friendship with him."

Elizabeth looked at the boys. None of them looked mean or nasty. They were just ordinary boys, the kind Richard should have associated with throughout his young life, instead of being hidden away at Allward, isolated from the world.

Elizabeth appealed to them. "Please, gentlemen, listen to me for a moment. I am Richard's aunt, Mrs. Drayton. If you can think of anything, no matter how far-fetched, that might relate to Richard's disappearance, please tell me. I will see to it that you are not blamed or punished. Please tell me if you have any glimmer of an idea, I beg you."

The only answer was silence, save for the sound of a couple of the boys sniffling and Mrs. Jones's muffled sobs. Mr. Harris paced, Mr. Macneil stared out of the window, Harry patted her shoulder, and Elizabeth dried a tear with her hankie. She tried to engage each of the boys, compel each one to meet her eyes. She was certain she would know if one of them had something to say. She noticed the smallest boy, in the farthest corner, kept glancing at her, then quickly looking away. She gave him a little smile, and he bent his head low. He looked like something was eating at his conscience.

She turned to the tutor. "Mr. Harris, can you dismiss them? Someone might speak to us if the others do not know about it."

He nodded. "You may go upstairs, boys, but please do not leave the building until I give you permission."

Some of them rushed away, others lingered. The little boy Elizabeth had singled out lagged behind the others, stealing a look at her from time to time. She rose and slowly walked out of the room and into the corridor, stepping toward the dimness behind the staircase.

The young man followed, beckoning her into the back stairwell where no one could see them.

"Do you have something to tell me? If so, I will honor your confidence."

"I am Philip Alister. No one is talking because we did something bad." He stopped and stared at the toes of his shoes.

"Go on, Philip. I will not repeat anything you say."

He heaved a deep breath. "Six of us snuck off last

Saturday to go to the fair. Out beyond the gates. We saw the signs around town."

"And Richard went with you?"

"Yes, we watched the wrestling and the man with the dancing bear. And a lady on stilts. And the monkey stole my hat."

"Did you come back here together?"

"Yes, Richard was here that night, but he was gone the next day after church. I do not think he came with us to church, but I cannot remember."

"And the other five of you promised not to tell?"

"We promised each other. We knew we would be punished if Mr. Harris or Mrs. Jones found out."

"Can you tell me the names of the other boys?"

Philip looked frightened, his eyes wide and his hands shaking. "Oh, no, Mrs. Drayton. I promised."

"But you might help us find Richard."

"None of them know any more than I do. He came back with us, but we did not see him the next morning. Please do not make me tell."

Elizabeth took pity on the lad. "For now, I will not, but you try to convince the others to come to me."

"Yes, ma'am."

He scooted away. Elizabeth leaned her head against the wall and tried to think. If Richard came back with the other boys, what did his visit to the fair signify?

She tried to visualize Richard and the boys at the fair. For Richard, it would have been a first. He had never been allowed to go to local markets or fairs. Hester and the dowager always feared the gypsies would carry him off.

Merciful heavens, could that have happened to Richard? Could a gypsy or some other ruffian have spotted the boys and followed them back to Mrs. Jones's, later finding a moment to entice one outside where he could be grabbed?

It was a possibility. Yet, it did not quite ring true. Richard would have screamed or yelled, and someone would have heard.

She walked back to the dining room where Mrs. Jones still snuffled into her handkerchief. Mr. Harris, Mr. Macneil, and Harry stood in silence. All of the boys had gone.

Elizabeth motioned to Harry, and they walked outside.

"I managed to convince one of the boys to tell me more." She related to Harry what Philip had said. "Do you think there is useful information there?"

Harry ran his hand through his hair. "Seems to me we want to find that fair."

Harry took Mr. Macneil and went to look for the performers at the fair. Elizabeth stayed behind to see if she could talk to any of the other boys or if Mrs. Jones could pull herself together.

Throughout the afternoon, as Elizabeth moved from one secluded area of the house to another, several boys whispered their confessions to her of their secret visit to the fair. It seemed a small thing, that little visit, but she was sure it held the key to Richard's disappearance. Elizabeth reassured each boy that his secret was safe with her.

The shadows were lengthening by the time Mrs. Jones was capable of talking. Or nearly capable, Elizabeth thought. The poor woman had shredded her linen handkerchief and rubbed her nose red. Probably in her sixties, Mrs. Jones wore a dress of practical dark gray wool and a white cap with a thin frill of lace. "Mrs. Drayton, I cannot tell you how sorry I am about the little earl's disappearance."

"Yes, Mrs. Jones. I know you want to see his safe return just as much as I do. What can you tell me about Richard and the other boys? Was he making friends?"

Mrs. Jones sniffed into a fresh hankie. "I tried to help him, such a solemn little fellow. His mama, the countess, sent me—"

"Yes, I heard about that letter."

"Oh, believe me, I did not mean to criticize. I know I should not have asked Mr. Macneil—"

"My sister-in-law should never have sent those instructions. Richard's upbringing has been far too harsh in my opinion, and if he has run away . . ." She stopped herself before she said any more. "Please go on, Mrs. Jones."

"I did not force him to read those essays every day. I cannot imagine what his mother will think."

Elizabeth learned little from Mrs. Jones. She had heard nothing during the night and declared she was a light sleeper. If anyone had broken in to grab him, she was convinced she would have heard it.

Harry and Mr. Macneil found no trace of the fair other than a few crumpled hand bills among the trash beside the road.

"The stupendous weight lifting of the Cornish Strongman . . . the hilarious antics of Capelli . . . Sigmund, the world's tallest man . . . the death-defying rope dancer . . ."

They inquired at the local inns, and, at the fourth, found the troupe.

Harry watched the innkeeper talk to a short fellow with a bulbous nose across the taproom. The man looked in Harry's direction, then got up and came over to their table.

"Josiah Nelson, proprietor of Nelson's Amazing Feats, at your service." He carried a mug and took a long swallow.

Harry gestured to the bench. "Have a seat, Mr.

Nelson. On last Saturday, your show was at the fair outside of Eton and Windsor."

"We was indeed, and a fine crowd we had. Sigmund was at his best and the—"

"Excuse me for interrupting, but we have an urgent task. Do you remember a bunch of young fellows, students over at Eton, who came to one of your shows?"

Nelson looked apprehensive. "Snuck out, did they?"

"Yes, they did, but of course you bear no responsibility for that."

"No, no, indeed. I believe I do recall those boys."

"Did any of them say or do anything that sticks in your mind?"

"A few of them always get to the show when we come to town. Don't remember any specifically. 'Cept that one came back on Sunday, as we was packing up. Li'l feller wanted to join up. I sent him packing, I tell ye. Told him he needed a gimmick, somethin' to make a show, learn to juggle . . . or get a monkey . . ."

"Did you see where he went?"

"Naw, sorry. We was busy . . ."

Harry wanted to slap his forehead for missing it. Now he remembered how he and Elizabeth had laughed when, at Astley's, Richard said he wished he could perform in such a show. Did not all young boys at some point want to run off and join a traveling troupe?

When Harry returned to Elizabeth and told her of Josiah's encounter with a young boy, he was careful not to influence her opinion, but she immediately jumped to the same conclusion. If Richard had come to Josiah on Sunday morning to join his troupe, he was only manifesting that boyhood dream of so many, she said, to run off and become an actor or a clown.

Without telling Mrs. Jones or Mr. Harris where they were headed, Elizabeth and Harry left Mr. Macneil to carry on a further search around Eton. If he had gone to Town to try and join up with Astley's, he might see the light at some point or run into enough difficulties that he would come back here.

As they rode back to Richmond, Elizabeth's head ached with the thought of one little boy, gone now for three days, somewhere near London. She longed to see him and prayed he would be at her house with Sally when they returned.

Her heart raced when she ran into the house, only to confront Sally's grim face. No words were necessary.

When Sally went home, dejected, Harry put his arms around Elizabeth and kissed her hair. "I'll head to London and see if he might have gone to Astley's. Meanwhile, just hope he comes here eventually."

She nodded. "Harry, I cannot thank you enough. I am certain your journey will be in vain and he will be here by morning."

"If he does come, send Jed with a message to my lodgings. I will check there during the day tomorrow and continue the search."

When he had gone, she tried to imagine where Richard could be. What if he were lost in the woods, or crouching in some copse of trees, or in the brush alongside the road? Or, God forbid, in some dark alley, hiding from the minions of the night?

If he had money, he might have tried to put up at an inn. But even the most respectable of inns would hardly be a safe place for a boy of nine. A truly respectable one would not even allow such a young person to stay there alone.

Before Elizabeth and Harry had left Eton, Harry

had sent a squad of four Eton porters out to scour nearby hostelries and ask people if they had seen the boy. Perhaps they would come up with some answers.

Just as Elizabeth finished a simple meal of soup, Mr. Iveson arrived. "My daughter told me about your nephew, Mrs. Drayton."

"I am very concerned about the boy."

"As you should be." The vicar settled into a chair and recalled his own memories of yearning to be an actor.

Elizabeth was only half listening, staring into the fire.

". . . and I wanted to have a monkey until I played with one, and it took a healthy chunk out of my arm."

Elizabeth snapped her gaze to Mr. Iveson. "A monkey!"

"Nasty little creatures."

She felt a swell of excitement. "Excuse me, Mr. Iveson, but I believe you just said something that could be important. When we saw a monkey at Astley's, Mr. Marlowe said something about a boy on his South American voyage getting a monkey. And that is one of the things the man who operates the Astounding Feats said to Harry. Something about telling Richard to get a monkey . . ."

"Are you saying the boy might have gone off to find a monkey?"

"Yes, but where would that be? How would you find a monkey?" Elizabeth sank back in her chair, looking dejected again. "We are right back where we started, with no idea where he could have gone."

"I suppose if you looked hard enough, you could find an animal seller someplace in London, but I have no idea where."

"Nor would he."

The vicar stared at the ceiling. "When I wanted to run away with the gypsies, I did not stop to consider the consequences. I just started running. Though I only got to the crossroads . . . a nine-year-old lad is ready to do anything."

"Do you suppose he might have tried to find a vessel bound for Brazil? That is where Mr. Marlowe saw the monkeys."

"That would take months, and how would he ever get home again?"

"But you just said he would not be thinking clearly. So, where would he go to board a ship? To Plymouth?"

"I think London is more likely."

Elizabeth jumped up and planted a kiss on the vicar's bald pate. "Mr. Iveson, this sounds better and better. I must write a note to Mr. Marlowe immediately."

Fifteen

Harry drove to Richmond thoroughly dejected. Though he had tried all day, he had not picked up Richard's trail in London. He had nothing to report to Elizabeth for his hours last night at Astley's and today at the docks. The only positive part of his efforts had been the half dozen men he hired to continue the search.

It would be dark when he arrived at Cloud Spring, but he had to get there, for Elizabeth would be terribly concerned if he did not get word to her. The last thing he wanted was to add to her fears. Unless, the thought came with a stab of hope, Richard had turned up. But Harry felt in his gut the boy was still missing.

For a moment, he wished he could grab Richard's shoulders and give him a shake. The boy should have thought before he set off about how others would worry. But he was only nine. More to the point was a hard shake for the boy's mother and several for his grandmother. Elizabeth would not have exaggerated the treatment meted out at Allward.

If he ever had a son, Harry mused as twilight fell on the Richmond Road, he would give him a normal upbringing. Tutors, yes. But also fun with other children. Sociability was an important ingredient of education.

He had always wished to be a father. Perhaps, if he

played his cards right, he still could have children. Elizabeth's sons would be strong and handsome, clever and caring. *Elizabeth's sons with me, that is.*

She also wanted children, or so she had said. All women wanted children, did they not? He must remember that fact when he was trying to convince her.

But first, Elizabeth wanted to be independent, a goal he could well understand. What must it have been for a young woman to be thrust into a marriage she did not choose, to end up in the bed of a man who was practically a stranger?

Elizabeth said she was fond of Reginald but expressed nothing like the passion he felt she had deep within her. Oh, she had passion, that he knew. When they had begun their sham betrothal, he had not expected that he would desire her, desire her as a wife.

He still attended the meetings to arrange the voyage for botanical specimens. He had contributed funds for it, and he would give more. But he no longer could envision himself going. He had even spoken to Owen Macneil about taking his place.

Yes, he was ready to drop his idea of taking another voyage and replace it with a bridal trip, somewhat shorter but infinitely more rewarding.

But he still had to bide his time, wait until the right moment to beg Elizabeth to abandon her idea of complete independence. He had been on the verge of suggesting it when Richard had disappeared. She could have her independence, her house and her garden, but he wanted to share it with her. He would not insist on making all the decisions. He was sure he could learn to respect her self-sufficiency. He loved her enough to do anything to persuade her. But not quite yet.

When he arrived at Cloud Spring, he could see lights in most of the windows. He had a sudden rush of hope that Richard was here, that he had been found. But when he hurried into the house, Elizabeth's look of anticipation, then the quick frown when she saw his gloomy face, told him they were both disappointed.

He sat down wearily and told her about his unsuccessful quest. Peg brought him a plate of hearty stew, sliced him a thick slab of bread, and poured him a glass of ale.

Elizabeth watched him eat. "You look exhausted."

"I am disappointed." He would not upset her by cataloging all the problems of hunting through the docks.

"I had an idea, Harry. What if Richard tried to get to London by river?"

Harry's brain felt foggy, but the idea struck him as reasonable. All sorts of traffic used the river, for centuries a great highway to move people and goods. Yes, it was a possibility. "I think you may have hit on an excellent idea, Elizabeth. I wonder if I should go back to London by river?"

"I think we should go by road. Even moving slowly on the river if he found a barge last Sunday, he would be at the docks by now. And you did not find him there."

"The docks are huge, there are hundreds, perhaps thousands of vessels, some moored out in the river. But did I hear you say *we*?"

"Yes, this time I must go along with you. I am certain that if he was making his way here on foot, he would have arrived by now. I cannot tolerate waiting here another day. I must help with the search."

Harry started to disagree but then thought better of it. If he was ever to convince her that he could respect her independence, he had to start now. "I understand. I will bed down at the hotel again and be back here shortly after dawn."

* * *

By the time they reached London the next morning, Elizabeth's nerves were ragged with tension. She searched every vehicle they passed, every face on the teeming roads and streets. To think of Richard alone and lost somewhere . . . It was almost more than she could bear.

They stopped at an inn near the Thames at the edge of the city, a run-down place where several poorly dressed men sat outside drinking from mugs. Though it was grandly titled the Crown and Anchor, one shutter hung crookedly, the windows were grimy, and it held the general air of dejection.

Harry asked the men where the riverboats were most likely to be found.

"Jest ahead, the smaller ones put up. And more'll be further along, between the big docks. They tend to stay together in clumps."

"Thank you, my man." Harry tossed him a coin and received a salute in return.

Elizabeth had never seen anything like the bustle and squalor of streets near the wharves. Though she wore her oldest black pelisse and a plain straw bonnet, she bore no resemblance to the women in sooty aprons who carried huge bundles or led heavily laden donkey carts along the streets. Dirty children played in the muddy puddles, and dozens of mangy dogs sniffed for stray morsels of food. Elizabeth shivered, not from the temperature.

Al stayed with the horses when they finally found the first cluster of riverboats, the first five or six wherries moored to pilings out in the river and another dozen rafted to them.

An appalling smell rose from the exposed tidal muck, from a mixture of rotting fish, the offal of countless butcher shops, the slimy contents of sewer pipes, the filthy runoff from the streets, all dumping into the great river to be washed out to sea.

Harry kept Elizabeth's arm linked through his as they walked toward the water. Buildings in an amazing variety stood side by side—the sturdy brick warehouses next to the flimsiest shack made of waterworn planks leaning on a wire. When Elizabeth and Harry came to the end of the street, amidst barrels and crates of all sizes and shapes, bundles wrapped in burlap, and coils of rope and chain, she looked up and down the river. On both sides, there were hundreds, thousands of boats, vessels of all sizes and shapes. How could they ever cover a fraction of them?

In deep water, tall merchant vessels with towering masts and spreading spars swung lazily from the anchor rodes. Skiffs rowed among boats and barges, a constant spectacle of movement on the oily water. Elizabeth could only stare, amazed at the contrast with the grassy slopes along the tree-lined river at Richmond. There she saw the beauty of the gentle stream dotted with wherries and barges. Here, the river reflected the splendor and squalor of the realm, the power of a great ship of the line, the insignificance of a rotting scow poling its way to a berth.

The only way they could reach many of the riverboats, tied together well out into the river, was to hire a skiff and have themselves rowed. Once out in the river, she caught a whiff of cinnamon and cloves from some trader loaded with spices, but the aroma did not last long.

They went from barge to wherry to coastal lighter, always asking the same question. "Has anyone seen a little boy of nine in a green coat?"

The answers varied from a polite "no" to drunken laughter. A boy here? Who would notice? Who would care? The docks and wharves stretched down river to

Greenwich and beyond. The search seemed hopeless. But Elizabeth would not give up. Nor would Harry.

In the early afternoon, Harry insisted they drive away from the docks and refresh themselves at a respectable inn. But once they had eaten, Elizabeth insisted they go back immediately, this time to try the other side of the river.

Again, they found a man to row them from craft to craft.

As the afternoon wore on, they questioned many and were rebuffed by others not interested in sharing information with their ilk. As Harry spoke to a man braiding lines, Elizabeth noticed a woman on a barge near the center of the cluster of boats tied together. As they moved from boat to boat, Elizabeth could see her looking in their direction, though whenever she tried to meet the woman's gaze, she looked away.

"We are looking for a young boy of about nine," Harry said again to another man, smoking a pipe as he sat on the gunnel of his barge. Elizabeth saw the man's eyes shift to the woman, then back.

"He has run away, we believe, and his mother is worried. I am offering a generous reward . . ."

Elizabeth watched the man glance over at the woman again and then wave his hand to cut off Harry's words.

"Naw. No boys 'round 'ere what don't belong. Notta one." He took the pipe from his mouth and spat into the river, shaking his head, then throwing one more look at the woman.

A similar exchange occurred at the next boat. Once again, their requests were shrugged off, but a glance or two at the woman, who continued to watch them, gave Elizabeth the distinct feeling they had found a clue to Richard's whereabouts.

She explained her supposition to Harry and after one more exchange that yielded no information but included furtive looks toward the woman, Harry agreed they must question her, though carefully.

The rower was able to maneuver their small boat a bit closer and they waved at the woman a few boats away. They could get no nearer.

"Ma'am, could we have a word with you?" Harry called to her.

She pointed to herself. "Me?"

"Yes, my good woman, if you please."

At first, she hesitated and Elizabeth feared they were out of luck. But suddenly the woman scrambled over the three intervening crafts until she stood immediately next to them.

"Wot kin I do fer ye?"

Elizabeth placed her hand on Harry's knee, and he nodded, deferring to her.

"I am Mrs. Drayton, and I live in Richmond. We are looking for my nephew, Richard, a boy of nine. He disappeared from the town of Eton, and we think he might have the idea of making his way to London and thence to find a ship, perhaps sailing for Brazil. Is there any possibility you might have seen him?"

The woman pursed her lips and stared at Elizabeth, then at Harry. "Wot you be wantin' to do with the lad, if'n ye find 'im?"

"Mr. Marlowe, here, and I want to be sure he is safe. He needs his family. His mother lives in Yorkshire, but we know she is upset, for he is her only child."

The scrutiny continued, as if the woman could assess their honesty if she memorized every detail of their appearance. "Brazil, ye say?"

"We think he was in search of a monkey, and Mr. Marlowe told him there were monkeys in Brazil."

Again, there was a long pause.

Elizabeth could not bear the tension. In her heart, she felt they were getting close. This woman had some information, she was certain.

"Believe me, ma'am, we love the boy and want only to help him, not punish him. We think he might have been bullied at school. He's a sensitive lad, raised without many friends, and he does not understand the raillery that goes on among boys." She felt a tear run down her cheek and fumbled for a handkerchief.

"'Ere, now. Don't bawl. If'n I knew where the lad was, where'd he find ye?"

Harry took Elizabeth's hand. "We'll be right here along the river. If we have to ask every person on the Thames, we shall not stop looking until he is found."

The woman nodded, gave them one more once-over, scrambled back to her previous perch, and disappeared under the canvas awning that sheltered the midsection of her vessel.

Elizabeth looked out at the river and noted several of the boatmen they had questioned suddenly shifting their eyes away. Many had been watching. She whispered to Harry. "I am sure she knows something."

"As am I. We'll stay in sight of her."

Harry gave instructions to the rower, who carried them farther along the boats.

Elizabeth felt she might snap with the tension of waiting. "I want to go after that woman and beg until she tells me. But that would not help."

Harry gave a grim nod.

Elizabeth looked again at the woman's wherry. "Why does she not help us? I can just feel that she knows something."

"These people are suspicious for good reason. They fish a precarious living out of this river, and around every bend there are scoundrels waiting to sink their little kingdoms. They have a need to be skeptical. Your good woman has no reason to trust us."

"But we are Richard's family . . ." Elizabeth knew this was no answer. But her insides churned, and she clamped her teeth on her lip until it hurt. Her head pounded and ears burned. Her back ached from sitting on the narrow plank that served as a seat; fumes from the river made her nauseated. The water under the oars swirled thick with debris, globs of unidentifiable trash, and she covered her eyes with her hands.

She felt helpless and hopeless. She dropped her head to her chest and tried to choke back the tears.

"Aunt Elizabeth! Mr. Marlowe!"

The voice came from a distance, but it was undoubtedly Richard.

Elizabeth turned and saw Richard waving as he stood beside the woman they had questioned. Harry saw him at the same moment and gave a shout, grabbing Elizabeth's arm to keep her from jumping to her feet.

Elizabeth waved and let her tears flow freely. The boatman gave one oar a mighty stroke. The boat swiveled around and skimmed back to the cluster of river barges.

The woman clambered toward them and grabbed the rope to tie them fast to the edge of a barge.

"Aunt Elizabeth! I am so happy to see you."

"Oh, Richard, where have you been?" Without a care for how awkwardly she managed it or whether her petticoat flew up over her knees, Elizabeth crawled from the rowboat to the barge and grabbed Richard to her. "Are you all right?"

"I just feel stupid."

"We have all been so worried about you, Mr.

Macneil and Mrs. Jones and your tutors and all the boys."

"I am sorry. I did not think anyone would care—"

Harry stepped onto the barge and ruffled Richard's hair. "You got started and then you were afraid to turn back?"

"I guess so. I wanted to . . . I wanted to . . ." Richard gave way to his tears and sobbed against Elizabeth.

Harry turned to the woman, who watched them through narrowed eyes. "Thank you for your help, ma'am."

Her grin revealed only a few teeth. "Miz Grimes, Birdy, they call me. Ready to head for the jungles, this lad said. But I figured someone'd be lookin'—quality the lad is, ain't he?"

"Yes, he's not used to the City."

"I knowt 'e was quality. He ain't for a life on the streets. Innocent, I said to Gerdy. Let him loose 'round here, he'd be fleeced in a minute, if not skinned alive or sold for a handful of groats."

"You are right, Mrs. Grimes. Absolutely right." Elizabeth looked up and wiped her eyes. "You kept him safe for us."

Harry wrote down her name and the name of her boat, the *Bluebird*. "The reward is twenty guineas. Do you want it now, or should I put it in a bank in your name?"

"Birdy don't take money for helping a boy. I jest did it for the good of the lad."

Elizabeth reached for her hand. "You must."

"I caint take yer money."

"Of course you can. Put it in the bank for your old age."

The woman wagged her head no. "Not Birdy."

They had to settle for giving her three guineas

and her promise to contact them if she was ever in need.

When they got into the carriage, Elizabeth continued to hug Richard tightly.

Richard's sobs had calmed. "Birdy, Mrs. Grimes, told me everyone would be looking for me. I did not think of that. Herbert threatened to tell that I made the young boys sneak away. And I do not know how to play cricket. And I cannot . . ." He broke again into sobs. "I thought I hated school, but I was afraid. . . . Please do not make me go back to Allward."

"You will not have to go anywhere you do not want to, Richard, if you promise not to run away ever again. Now, we must hurry to Alice's house and send word to your mother immediately."

"Do you have to tell her?"

"She already knows you went missing from Eton. We thought you might try to make your way to Yorkshire."

"I wanted to have a monkey and do tricks at the fair."

When messages were dispatched to Yorkshire and Eton, Alice and Elizabeth oversaw a warm bath, supper, and bed for Richard.

Elizabeth turned down the light and gave him a good night kiss. "Promise never to run away?"

"I promise."

She paused and watched him snuggle into the soft feather mattress. He was asleep in an instant.

In the drawing room, Harry and Blaine poured celebratory glasses of wine.

Harry swirled his glass and stared into its ruby depths. "Despite his foolish behavior, he used amazing good sense to head for London by river. Did he say how he found Mrs. Grimes?"

Elizabeth slipped her feet out of her slippers. "He went to the river and tried to tell the boatmen he'd been beaten and left behind by his family. Most of them thought he was crazy, but she believed his story, at least until he started talking about Brazil. She told him she was taking him right back upriver as soon as they got their new load."

Alice rang for the tea tray.

Elizabeth could not stifle a yawn. "Harry, I cannot thank you enough for helping me find him."

"You had all the good ideas, Elizabeth. And did all the convincing talk. Now, I think you are way behind on your sleep, my dear. As am I. So, I will say good night."

Elizabeth walked him to the door. "Harry, you are the kindest and most reliable man I have ever known."

He placed a light kiss on her hand. "And you are the cleverest and most beautiful lady."

When she went upstairs, Elizabeth thought once more how lucky she was to have Harry for a friend. And how unlucky their betrothal was only a pretense.

By midafternoon the next day, Elizabeth, Harry, and Richard turned up the driveway at Cloud Spring. Elizabeth took a long look at her house, happy to be returning to it with Richard beside her. But what was that tall traveling carriage doing there?

With a sinking heart, she recognized it as belonging to Allward.

She could see Hester pacing beside the vehicle, then stopping and squinting until she saw Richard in the carriage. "Oh, oh," she screamed. "My Richard!"

The carriage had hardly rolled to a halt before the boy leaped out and into his mother's arms.

The dowager, peering through the coach window, wore her usual frown. Elizabeth went over to her. "Lady Allward. We have found Richard. Will you not come in?"

The old countess narrowed her eyes. "How far has news of this affair traveled? I do not wish our family name to be associated with gossip."

Elizabeth shook her head in wonder. Gossip was her first concern?

"I also hope you have reprimanded him for frightening his mother. I have a few words to say—"

Elizabeth held up a hand to stop her. "No! There will be no punishments for him in my house! He is safe, and that is all that matters."

"And what *is* the meaning of this house, Elizabeth?"

"I will tell you about it later. Do you not wish to get out of the coach and give him a kiss? He is very concerned that everyone was worried about him."

"He should have thought of that before he ran away."

Elizabeth turned her back on the dowager and watched Hester cuddle her son. The old woman's meanness was the source of Richard's difficulties with Eton.

Mr. Macneil brought Elizabeth's cob to a halt, jumped down, and ran to Richard and his mama. Harry grabbed the reins and, with a wry glance at Elizabeth, led the animal toward the stables.

Elizabeth motioned to the groom, still sitting up beside the coachman. "Help Lady Allward out, please, and take her into the house."

Elizabeth joined the happy reunion of Richard, Hester, and Mr. Macneil.

Sixteen

When Elizabeth awoke on Thursday morning, she opened her eyes slowly, almost afraid to see the dawn. Then the events of the previous days flooded her memory, and she hugged herself with relief. She slept on a couch in her studio, having given the bedrooms to Richard, Hester, and the dowager. Elizabeth tiptoed into her bedchamber, eager to lay her eyes again on Richard. He slept deeply, looking angelic, as if he could never have caused anyone the slightest concern for his welfare.

As she dressed, she wondered how best to celebrate his return. The dowager, in her unbending way, insisted that she would leave this morning. Hester would go to Eton to spend a few days with her son, then stay in London with her aunt, perhaps not returning to Allward for some months.

Elizabeth went downstairs and found the dowager already dressed in traveling clothes.

"I shall depart as soon as I have another talk with Richard. Although I have never been able to rely on you, Elizabeth, to do your duty by my family, I have instructions for you regarding the boy and Hester."

"For me?" Elizabeth was surprised, knowing the woman's disdain for her. Why would she bother to ask for help?

"Hester is too soft. She is easy on the boy, and I

want to prevent him from becoming like her. If you have any loyalty at all to your late husband, you must oversee my instructions regarding Richard's education and his constitution. He needs to be stronger. I was remiss in that regard."

"Boys grow at different rates—"

"I believe he should swim daily, in the coldest water nearby. I have read such a regime will strengthen young boys."

Or cause them life-threatening chills, Elizabeth thought.

The dowager took a folded sheet of paper from her reticule. "Last night, I listed more instructions for you. Hester will have the same list, but I do not believe that she, without my guidance, will carry through on them. I am sorry to say I must rely upon you to encourage her and to deal with the authorities at Eton. Now that they know Richard's unfortunate tendencies for fantasy, they will have to be harder on him. I have written to the headmaster to find a replacement for Mr. Macneil, who proved unreliable and forfeited any right to see Richard ever again."

"But Mr. Macneil did everything he could to help find Richard."

"He should have watched more closely. I will not revoke my husband's instructions for his heirs to attend Eton, however poorly I think they have treated the Earl of Allward. They have not done their duty."

Elizabeth took the instructions. She burned with rage, though she tried to speak with reason. "Lady Allward, do you not understand that what made Richard run away was his overly strict upbringing? He needs to learn to make friends, not follow rules that set him apart from the other boys. He needs companions and mentors like Mr. Macneil."

"Do not mention that man's name. I will see that he never gets a position of responsibility again."

Elizabeth could not believe what she heard. "Lady Allward, I think you have the problem backward. Completely turned around. You say you have no respect for me. Well, let me say that I have no respect for what you have done for Richard. And for Hester. Instead of a normal boy's upbringing, he has been raised without friends. He did not know how to act around the other boys. And Hester, poor woman, has been mistreated by you, probably since she was a bride."

The dowager's eyes glittered. "I see my suspicions about you have been correct from the start, Elizabeth. You were never worthy of Reginald, and now you dishonor his name and that of our family. I will not contest Reginald's legacy to you. It would be a scandal that everyone would talk about. I cannot stop you from making a disgusting spectacle of yourself with that man."

Elizabeth had enough. "Stop! I do not care what you think of me anymore. However, I will not allow you to impugn Mr. Marlowe's good name. His conduct is above reproach. As is mine. So, cease this harangue and leave my house. If you wish to wait in your carriage until Richard can see you, he and Hester can come out and wish you good-bye. But Richard does not need another of your lectures. Lady Allward, I think you have a very strange sense of what is right for a child. He needs love and kindness."

The dowager stood, her eyes flashing with anger. "Mark my words—"

"No! Your words are not welcome, and I will not listen to one more."

Elizabeth stalked outside and ordered the carriage brought to the doorstep. When she returned to the house, Sally beckoned to her from the drawing room.

"I did not mean to intrude, but I came to see if I could help you and overheard your . . . your, ah, conversation with the dowager. You were magnificent, Elizabeth. You were not disrespectful, but you told her where things stand."

Elizabeth's hands still shook from the tension of the exchange. "Thank you, my dear. I did not mean to lose my temper, but I could not stop."

"She was impossible. You have been waiting a long time to speak up, am I correct?"

"Too long."

"Mr. Marlowe will be proud that it was a slur on his name that set you off."

"Do not dare to tell him that!"

"But it is true."

"Sally Iveson!"

Sally laughed. "I do not promise to keep mum."

Elizabeth smiled for the first time in the last half hour. "I cannot make you. But Sally, I have something for you to do. I want to have a party to celebrate Richard's return. Can you help me make a list of people to invite, such as the neighbors nearby? Then, we will need to hire some extra servants. Peg will know of some, perhaps. And we need to write a menu. Nothing fancy, but some special cakes perhaps. And Mr. Marlowe is partial to crab puffs. Or is it lobster?"

"Why not have both? I will go to the kitchen and get started immediately."

"As soon as the dowager is gone, I will write to my cousins, the Powells, and Mr. Macneil. Perhaps Mr. Harris and Mrs. Jones can bring all the boys for an afternoon."

"We can organize a three-legged race and lots more games."

"Thank you, my dear." Elizabeth patted the girl's shoulder.

"It sounds like the best fun in weeks."

By the time Elizabeth returned to the dining room, the dowager sat ramrod straight, her face a grim mask.

"Your carriage is here, ma'am. I want you to know I bear you no ill will. If you begin to live normally again, I beg you to contact me. Your son Reginald will always be high in my esteem. And the earl and Hester will always have my love and support."

The dowager's only response was a frosty grimace. She turned and marched out of the house, unbending to the end.

It was not easy convincing Hester and Richard to climb into her coach a quarter hour later to make their good-byes.

"Hester," Elizabeth said. "You must not let her mistreat the boy. When she starts lecturing him, just take his hand and climb out."

"But she always . . ."

"You can be strong, Hester. I know you can. What she did to Richard was wrong, and now you must help correct the situation. Do not let her frighten him anymore."

"I know you have the right of it. But I have never been able to find my voice against her. Even when I saw how hard things were for Richard." She began to weep.

"Crying will not help him now, Hester. Please wipe your eyes and be strong."

Hester drew a deep, shuddering breath. "I shall try."

Richard came in from the breakfast room and took his mother's hand.

Elizabeth did not ask them when they returned ten minutes later just what had been said. But Hester wore a weak smile with her tears. Best of all, Richard was not crying.

They all watched as the dowager's coach turned onto the road.

Elizabeth exchanged a smile with Hester. "Now, Richard, we have a party to plan."

When Serena arrived in a hired carriage accompanied by Peter Rowley, the party was well underway. The lawn was dotted with boys playing games, and the garden was full of people enjoying the sunshine and lemonade. Elizabeth rushed over to welcome the new arrivals. "Peter, you were very helpful, and I am so grateful to you."

"It was my honor to assist. I am glad your search turned out to be so successful. I admit I was worried the result might be different."

"Your poor little nephew!" Serena threw her arms around Elizabeth. "You must have been frantic."

"I was. But it is over now, and he has earned a kind of respect from his fellow students for his adventure."

Serena gave a carefree laugh. "How very wonderful!"

She wore a white gown with several fringed scarves wrapped around her shoulders. The sunshine gave her hennaed hair a pink glow. Elizabeth could see many heads turned Serena's way.

Peter drew Elizabeth aside. He held a small satchel. "Can I ask your indulgence for a few moments?"

"Of course you can."

Serena waved to Harry and set off toward him.

Elizabeth and Peter went into the library. He removed two sheets of heavy paper from his satchel and spread out two watercolors on the desk. They were done from sketches he had made of her before she heard of Richard's disappearance. Both were excellent likenesses.

"Oh, Peter, these are superb. I am amazed you could do this by memory."

"I was worried about you. So, I tried to exert all my energy on these pictures until I heard your nephew was safe."

"I am very impressed with your ability, Peter. You have a great future."

"Thank you." He replaced them, and Peter and Elizabeth went back to the party.

The boys played ball on the lawn and chased each other around the trees. Elizabeth watched long enough to see that Richard participated fully, accepted at last.

Later, the adults laughed as they watched the boys attack the cold collation put together by Peg and her friends.

Elizabeth found Philip, the small boy who had come to her first with information about the surreptitious trip to the fair, and she gave him her special thanks. He was very relieved that Richard was safe and also glad his indiscretion remained a secret.

Elizabeth tried not to notice where Serena and Harry stood, whether they were close together or far apart, whether he smiled at her or touched her arm, but Elizabeth could not help watching them eating together. The sight gave her a pang of envy. Just as Serena had at her party, she had entwined her arm with his and leaned against him, gazing up into his eyes.

As though a black cloud blotted out the sun, Elizabeth's view darkened.

She watched them walk behind the house and out of sight. Feeling empty inside, her pulse grinding with a sad beat, she hastened inside to the library window. They ambled up the hill into the trees and out of sight. She wanted to run after them, demand they break apart.

But what right had she to tell either one of them what to do? She sat and put her head down on her desk, pushing Peter's satchel aside. Harry had no obligation to her at all, none whatsoever. And she had none to him.

Except the void where her heart should be now told her differently.

She felt a tear on her cheek and blotted it swiftly.

Wherever Harry went, to Brazil or Chile or Australia, she had abrogated all rights to him. Had she not clearly expressed her intention to be independent?

Just this morning, he had congratulated her on bringing her dreams to fruition.

But she had not told him how those dreams of self-reliance had changed. She treated Harry as a friend, a companion, and as a collaborator in the search for Richard. *But that is the real sham!*

She had done the unthinkable. She had lost her heart to Harry Marlowe. The pretend betrothal had turned upside down.

Worse yet, it looked like Harry might be losing his heart to Serena Stevens. Elizabeth herself had been entirely responsible for them knowing one another. If she had not asked him to escort her . . .

From what Elizabeth had seen of Serena's life, she probably collected men like some women collected gloves or bonnets. One for every new outfit. Serena had shown an interest in Harry right from the start. And why not? He was handsome in a rugged way, a rugged way that would no doubt appeal to Serena.

Elizabeth shrugged. Why be coy? A rugged way that appealed to her.

He had a charming manner. The fact that he

cared little for Society would be another plus to Serena. As it was to Elizabeth herself.

She sat up and gazed out of the window again. She saw only the gentle movement of the leaves in the breeze.

Face it, Elizabeth, you know nothing of love anyway. What you think is love might be as wispy as Serena's transparent scarves. What have you ever known of love?

After many years of marriage, she had respected Reginald. She had been fond of him, found his company more than tolerable, if hardly exciting. Reginald was never much of a conversationalist, especially after they went to Allward and lived under the rule of his mother. She supposed she loved him in a way. She appreciated his legacy and the independence it brought her.

And that was exactly the sticking point. Now that she had achieved her independence and everything she dreamed of was within reach, she found she wanted more.

She wanted Harry. And it felt very much like it was love, the kind of love the poets write of, the kind she was simply too dense to recognize until it was too late.

Another thing the poets wrote about was sacrifice. If love was true, then to sacrifice for the benefit of a lover was a kind of special honor. Apparently, honor would have to be her reward. For if she loved Harry, she would have to sacrifice her own heart's desire so that he could have his.

"Elizabeth!" Someone called, and she realized she was ignoring her duties as hostess.

"I am coming." She wiped her eyes, stood, and threw back her shoulders. She had declared she wanted independence, and now she had it.

She would tell Harry they should end their charade. If he wanted to pursue his interest in Serena, he should do so and follow it to whatever end he wanted.

Even if it meant Elizabeth would not see him anymore.

The day after the party, Elizabeth felt like the crumbled remains of the lobster puffs. In pieces. Shredded. Without substance.

Alice and Blaine came from the hotel for breakfast with Richard and Hester before going back to London. Mr. Macneil had arranged accommodations in Eton for Hester until she saw Richard settled. Then she would go to her aunt in Chelsea with an open invitation to return to Cloud Spring whenever she wished.

Elizabeth kept up a cheery mien until she had wished everyone good-bye.

Sally arrived just after Elizabeth changed into her old gardening dress, already dirtied beyond repair.

Sally chattered about the party, then stopped and placed her hand on Elizabeth's arm. "I did some spying yesterday."

"Spying?"

"Yes, at your party. I saw Mr. Marlowe and that lady with the awful hair go off alone."

"Sally, you should not have done that. And I certainly do not want to hear such things." Of course, Elizabeth very much wanted to hear whatever Sally said, but she was also afraid of what she would learn.

"I do not like that lady. She was clinging to him like burrs to a donkey's tail. Corky growled at her."

Elizabeth picked up her gardening gloves, a basket, and scissors. "I am going to the garden. You may come along if you stop talking such nonsense."

Sally walked beside her. "I thought you should

know that woman who calls you her friend went into the woods with your husband-to-be."

Elizabeth knew it was neither the time nor the place to attempt an explanation of her agreement with Harry. She said nothing, afraid to hear what Sally would tell next, but equally unwilling to cut her off.

"I followed them, but I stayed out of sight. They never saw me."

Elizabeth cut a faded bloom from a rosebush.

Sally went on. "When they stopped near the grotto, she tried to kiss him. But he kept stepping away from her."

Elizabeth paused and looked at Sally, then realized her mouth was agape. She turned back to the rosebush.

"Believe me, Mrs. Drayton, I was surprised too. I guessed he would give her at least one little kiss. But he did not."

Elizabeth stooped to pick up the forlorn blooms and put them in the basket.

"I could hear them talking. He told her about your idea to put a little fern garden near the grotto. And then he walked down the path that winds up right here." Sally dramatically swept her hand wide, indicating the entire garden. "All he talked about were your plans to plant things, and he knew all the names of them."

In spite of herself, Elizabeth could not help giving a little laugh, thinking about how Serena might have felt about this recitation of botanical information in Latin. Back in school, Serena never showed the slightest interest in the feeble attempts of their classics teacher.

"Sally, I know you thought you were doing what was best, but I do not think it was wise. You would not want to be spied upon when you thought you were alone."

"Oh, I know I should not have done it, but I was afraid she was going to trap him or something. And now I think you should know he did not succumb to her wiles."

"As punishment, I want you to take this scissors and cut off all the dead blooms. While you are doing so, think how you would feel if you were spied upon. And what you will do if I decide to tell your parents."

"Oh, Mrs. Drayton, say you won't do that, please."

Elizabeth grinned. "Well, I might be convinced if you do a very thorough job here."

Sally took the scissors and basket.

Elizabeth went back to the house for a second scissors. She stood in the back entry for several moments thinking. Harry had not kissed Serena in the woods, but that did not mean he was not interested in her. The conclusion of the party was almost a blur in her mind. She remembered saying good-bye to everyone until only Harry and those staying at Cloud Spring one more night were left.

Serena and Peter had gone in the midst of a crowd of departures.

Sally's revelations made no particular difference to the situation, even if the sick feeling in Elizabeth's heart was lightened. She still had to give Harry his freedom.

She hunted for a scissors but could not find another pair. As she went outside again, she heard Harry call out to the stable man to take his horse. At least she would not have to wait a long time before confronting him. She began the day by sending her mother-in-law out of her life. Apparently, she would end the day by sending her pretend fiancé away too.

Seventeen

Elizabeth tried to stay calm while she told Harry the news of the day's departures, though her pulse raced at what was to come. When they went into the garden, Sally handed her the basket of dead rose blossoms.

"Did I do a good enough job, Mrs. Drayton?"

Elizabeth looked around the garden. Sally seemed to have found all the blossoms that needed removal.

"Yes, I believe you have done well enough to earn the reprieve I promised you."

"What reprieve?" Harry asked.

"It is something just between Sally and me." She turned again to the young lady. "Now, clip a few of the nicest buds and take them to your mother. And remember, if such a situation arises again, you must resist the temptation to pry."

When she was gone, Harry spoke. "What was that all about?"

Elizabeth shrugged. "Sometimes, Sally forgets the Golden Rule. That is all I have to say about it."

"I asked Jed to bring the plants up to the place we chose for the fernery."

"What plants?"

"Do you really want to know? There are about a dozen *Phyllitis scolopendrium,* or hart's tongue fern. And another dozen *Polystichum setiferum.* As soon as they are established, they will spread. Then, I have a few *Dryopteris*—"

"Enough! Those names spill easily from your brain, but mine is not so nimble."

"Shall we go and have a look?" He reached for her hand and drew it under his arm.

She ought to stop him right now, tell him he was free to head straight for Fitzroy Square, if he wished. But he looked so eager to plant those ferns. . . .

She stumbled on a stone in the path, and Harry grabbed her tight. "Careful there, my dear."

"I am all right. I just hit a rock."

She almost laughed, hearing her own words. Yes, she hit a rock. The big old rock of her heart's desire.

Jed was already in the chosen spot with the wheelbarrow full of ferns. They were feathery and beautiful, like little plumes of lacy green. She lifted a little pot and took a closer look, letting the fronds tickle her cheeks.

Harry explained to Jed how he wanted the plants placed. "I'd like to have those three big rocks moved here, to form a little curve to counterbalance the stream. Can you move those, Jed?"

"Fer that, sir, I'll have ta git my cuzzin tomorrow. We kin do it."

"Then let us wait until the next day to plant these. We can leave them over here in the shade for now." He looked around the little glen. "You will want to place a bench here and a sort of rustic arch of willow branches . . ."

As he described the garden, it took shape in Elizabeth's mind. But she might have to oversee the work herself.

Jed unloaded the ferns and pushed his wheelbarrow back toward the shed.

Harry peered at the moss here and at the depth of the decaying leaves there. "This will be a very effective fernery, I think. In the fall, we can plant some bulbs and primroses amongst the ferns. The soil appears rich and damp."

Elizabeth wondered how she could bring up the topic, but her head felt as empty as her heart.

Eventually, he noticed she was simply standing there saying nothing. "Elizabeth, are you all right? My dear, you must be tired."

She shook her head. "That is not it. But, Harry, we must talk. Can we go back to the house?"

"If that is what you wish."

"Yes, please."

"What concerns you, Elizabeth?"

"We need to clarify things."

She picked up her skirts so that she could walk faster, and Harry followed, vaguely troubled by the look on her face. Now that Richard was back and he had talked to Mr. Macneil about the voyage, Harry wanted to begin courting Elizabeth for real. She was all he wanted, and although he wished to respect her notions of independence, he did not want to wait several years to have her.

Their sham betrothal started as a whim. But now he felt entirely different. First, his supposed longing to return to South America had evaporated into thin air. Just as he had been about to share his change of plans with Elizabeth, Richard had disappeared.

They took off their muddy shoes and went into the house. A frown furrowed Elizabeth's brow, and he wanted to take her in his arms and kiss it away. But she led the way to her library and sat in one chair, gesturing him to the other.

Elizabeth spoke first. "I do not know how to begin this discussion, Harry, except to begin. I think it is time we ended the charade of our pretend betrothal."

Words choked in his throat. "Go on."

She stared at the bookshelves. "I believe you should have the right to court others. You helped me find Richard, and you have been all that is kind in helping with this house. You have done so many things for me. I am grateful to you beyond words."

"I felt the loss of Richard as you did, very deeply indeed. I will forever thank heaven we were successful. Everything else I have done has been for my own enjoyment as well as yours."

"You are a generous man."

"Thank you." He paused for a deep breath. "I, too, want to change the status of our arrangement."

Her eyes snapped to his, wide and surprised, but her tone was quiet, almost sad. "Then, you do want to pursue others? Serena?"

"Take up with Serena?" He could not stop a burst of laughter. "Me? With Serena? I cannot imagine a more mismatched couple."

Elizabeth's voice grew tremulous. "But does she not appeal to you?"

He pulled his chair closer to hers. "Elizabeth, you cannot be serious. Serena is interesting, beyond my usual acquaintances. But when I talked to her, I was trying to find out more about you. She told me all about your girlhood, and I loved listening."

"But she is so . . . fascinating. And I am so . . . dull."

"Do I need to tell you I find you perfect? Serena belongs in her world. I belong in yours, right here in Richmond, trimming roses and planting ferns."

Elizabeth's eyes shone with tears. But her smile was broad.

Harry dared not stop. "Will you marry me, become my wife?"

"What?" She nearly hopped out of her chair. "What are you saying?"

"That I want our betrothal to be a real thing. I have decided Owen Macneil can take my place on the voyage. When he returns, we can work together with the specimens."

"Are you certain?"

"Yes, I decided weeks ago, but I did not want to tell you because you would worry how to end our pretense, our sham betrothal."

"But . . ."

"Many of my experiments would be ruined, and my bromeliads might die without me to care for them. I do not relish years of discomfort, not when I could be here at Cloud Spring with the lady I love."

A tear trickled down her cheek. "I do not know what to say."

He reached over to brush it away. "You do not need to say anything yet. I have more to say. I want Mr. Iveson to post the banns at St. Mary Magdalene, and I want us to have another party, this one without the Eton students, to proclaim our love to all our friends, the entire ton, if you wish. Lady Addie and Mrs. Welk can lead the applause when we announce the date of our wedding. And our scheming relatives can indeed have the last laugh."

"And you really do not care about Serena?"

He stood and drew her into his arms. "Not a fig, but I am delighted to hear your little twinge of envy. It bodes well for us becoming one of those couples for whom Society has sincere disdain because they are so obviously in love—and they stay in love, providing no grist for the gossip mills!"

Elizabeth put her arms around him and pressed near. "Harry, I think you should stop talking now and kiss me."

He did as he was told.